MW01100212

Elfreda the Saxon

EMMA LESLIE CHURCH HISTORY SERIES

Glaucia the Greek Slave
A Tale of Athens in the First Century

The Captives
Or, Escape From the Druid Council

Out of the Mouth of the Lion
Or, The Church in the Catacombs

Sowing Beside All Waters
A Tale of the World in the Church

From Bondage to Freedom
A Tale of the Times of Mohammed

The Martyr's Victory
A Story of Danish England

Gytha's Message
A Tale of Saxon England

Leofwine the Monk
Or, The Curse of the Ericsons
A Story of a Saxon Family

Elfreda the Saxon
Or, The Orphan of Jerusalem
A Sequel to Leofwine

Dearer Than Life
A Story of the Times of Wycliffe

Before the Dawn
A Tale of Wycliffe and Huss

Faithful, But Not Famous
A Tale of the French Reformation

The Dismissal of Elfreda

EMMA LESLIE CHURCH HISTORY SERIES

Elfreda the Saxon

Or, The Orphan of Jerusalem

A Sequel to Leofwine

BY

EMMA LESLIE

Illustrated by
D. H. FRISTON, FELTER, SHEERES & SYMMONS S.C.

Salem Ridge Press
Emmaus, Pennsylvania

Originally Published
1875
Nelson & Phillips

Republished 2009
Salem Ridge Press LLC
4263 Salem Drive
Emmaus, Pennsylvania 18049

www.salemridgepress.com

Hardcover ISBN: 978-1-934671-23-8
Softcover   ISBN: 978-1-934671-24-5

PUBLISHER'S NOTE

In *Elfreda the Saxon*, Emma Leslie has given us a powerful reminder of the complete misery that comes from trying to gain peace and forgiveness of sins apart from the finished work of Christ. While the "Curse of the Ericsons" is ultimately proven to have been a blessing, each one of us, like Guy and Elfreda, is born under the very real curse of sin, and despite our best efforts, each one of us is powerless to overcome it.

As a sequel to *Leofwine the Monk*, *Elfreda* is also a wonderful reminder of the blessing of a godly heritage. The greatest gifts that we, like Leofwine, can pass on to future generations are our prayers and the Word of God.

My prayer is that no matter what our situation, each of us will place our complete dependence on the Lord Jesus Christ, and also work to lay a godly foundation for many generations to come.

Daniel Mills

August, 2009

NOTE: Prejudice against the Jews, as depicted in this story, is a sad fact of history. Salem Ridge Press in no way approves of this prejudice in any form.

HISTORICAL NOTES

A number of important historical figures from the twelfth and thirteenth centuries A.D. are mentioned in *Elfreda the Saxon*. Here is a brief summary of some of these people:

Saladin: Born in the city of Tikrit in modern-day Iraq in A.D. 1138, Saladin was educated in Damascus by his uncle, Nur ad-Din, ruler of Syria. In A.D. 1171, at the age of thirty-three, Saladin gained control of Egypt, ruling it in the name of his uncle. When Nur ad-Din died three years later, Saladin became the Sultan of Egypt and Syria. A brief truce with the crusaders allowed Saladin to consolidate his rule, and then in A.D. 1179, he launched new attacks, culminating with the capture of Jerusalem in A.D. 1187.

King Richard I: In A.D. 1173, Richard joined with two of his brothers in an unsuccessful attempt to overthrow their father King Henry II. In A.D. 1189, Richard, now allied with King Philip II of France, attacked again, forcing Henry to proclaim Richard as his heir. Henry soon died and Richard was crowned King of England. Richard, Philip and King Leopold of Austria, enraged by Saladin's capture of Jerusalem, departed on the Third Crusade. Richard captured the stronghold of Acre but then quarreled with Philip and Leopold, causing both of them to abandon the Crusade. Richard continued the fight against Saladin but was unable to gain a decisive victory. At last, he signed a peace treaty with Saladin, leaving Jerusalem under Muslim control but allowing Christian pilgrims access to the city. Traveling back to England, Richard was captured and held for ransom by Leopold. Richard's mother raised the money required and Richard was released, returning to England in A.D. 1194. Richard died five years later while besieging a castle in central France.

William Longbeard: In the spring of A.D. 1196, William Fitz Osbern, a Saxon known as "Longbeard," led the poor of London in a revolt against oppression. The revolt was quickly put down and William Longbeard was executed.

Dominic de Guzman: Dominic was born in Spain in A.D. 1170. He founded the Dominican order of Friars to combat the heresy that he believed threatened the church. Dominic died in A.D. 1221 at the age of fifty-one.

Count Raymond VI: Raymond became Count of Toulouse, a city in southern France, in A.D. 1194. Because of the religious freedom that he allowed, Raymond was declared a heretic by the pope and a crusade was sent against him in A.D. 1209. Raymond fled to England and later, through several military campaigns, was able to recover his lands.

HISTORICAL NOTES

Simon de Montfort: The son of a French nobleman, Simon joined the Fourth Crusade in A.D. 1199, but abandoned it when the crusaders turned against towns held by Greek Orthodox Christians. Later, in A.D. 1209, Simon was appointed head of the crusade against Count Raymond. He defeated Raymond and ruled southern France for almost a decade, but was killed in battle while attempting to stop Raymond from recovering his lands.

King John: John was the youngest son of King Henry II of England. During Richard's absence on the Third Crusade, he seized control of England. Following Richard's death, John did become king, but a conflict with King Philip cost him control of northern France. Then, a disagreement with Pope Innocent III over the election of the Archbishop of Canterbury caused the pope to turn against him, and in A.D. 1213, John was forced to yield control of his kingdom to the pope. These failures lead to growing anger among the English barons and in A.D. 1215, they forced John to sign the *Magna Charta*, a legal document limiting the power of all future English monarchs.

Stephen Langton: Langton, a native Englishman, was appointed Archbishop of Canterbury in A.D. 1207 by the pope but John refused to accept Langton's appointment until A.D. 1213. Langton sided with the barons in forcing King John to sign the *Magna Charta*.

HISTORICAL NOTES

Founded in the early twelfth century, the **Knights Templar** was a organization of knights who took vows as monks for the purpose of defending pilgrims traveling to the Holy Land. Taking their name from their headquarters on the Temple Mount in Jerusalem, they grew in popularity and influence and were granted freedom from all local laws and taxes by the pope. Due to this freedom, they became wealthy and powerful, owning businesses and large amounts of land throughout Europe. By the end of the thirteenth century, they were coming under attack from jealous European rulers, and in A.D. 1312, the Knights Templar was officially disbanded by the pope. Most of their property was then transferred to the **Knights Hospitaler**, a similar organization founded for the purpose of running a hospital in Jerusalem for pilgrims. The military arm of the Knights Hospitaler also provided protection for the pilgrims.

IMPORTANT DATES

A.D.

1170 Murder of Thomas à Becket, Archbishop of
        Canterbury

1187 Saladin conquers Jerusalem

1189 Richard I crowned King of England

1190 Richard I begins the Third Crusade

1199 John becomes King of England

        Count Thibaut begins the Fourth Crusade

1203 Constantinople falls to the crusaders

1209 Simon de Montfort leads the crusade
        against southern France

1213 John surrenders his kingdom to the pope

1215 Signing of the *Magna Charta*

Europe in the 13ᵗʰ Century

The Eastern Mediterranean

CONTENTS

ILLUSTRATIONS

Elfreda the Saxon

Elfreda the Saxon

Chapter 1

Lady de Valery

"YES, I am Saxon, unmistakably Saxon," and the lady sighed as she glanced at her fair, shapely, but not very small hands and feet.

She lifted her eyes from her offending hands in a minute or two, and looked across the undulating pastures to the woods beyond. From her elevated position on the turret of her castle-home she could see every object for miles around, and she gazed long and steadfastly at the curling wreaths of smoke that rose from an irregular group of buildings on the edge of the distant wood. "I wonder, I wonder—" she began, but there she suddenly stopped, for one of her bower-maidens drew near, and the Lady de Valery would not have one of her attendants overhear her self-communing for half her jewels. She fondly thought that they believed

UNDULATING: *rolling*
BOWER-MAIDENS: *lady's maids*
SELF-COMMUNING: *talking to herself*

she was a Norman, and not one of the despised race whom the conquerors of England had made "hewers of wood and drawers of water" when they proclaimed themselves masters of the soil; but if her servants and attendants did not know that the long, low-roofed farmhouse just within view was her childhood's home, the lady herself never forgot it, nor her haughty lord either, although both were careful to conceal the fact from the knowledge of their children. Sometimes a wish had entered the lady's heart that the old homestead would be burned down in one of the quarrels that were perpetually occurring between the followers of the two families, for her brother as heartily despised the Norman usurpers of the land as they did the conquered race, and into this feeling theows and house-carls, lithsmen and pages, entered, each espousing the cause of his master, and showing his enmity to the other upon every possible occasion.

Sir Valence de Valery would, doubtless, have preferred that the humble home of his beautiful wife had been at a greater distance from his lordly castle; but he was too true a knight to take any mean advantage, or allow his followers to do more than carry off a few head of cattle or sheep by way of reprisals for some infringement of his rights as lord of the woods and plains from Crowland minster to the village of Bourne.

THEOWS: *slaves*
HOUSE-CARLS: *household men-servants*
LITHSMEN: *mercenary troops from the shipmen's guild*
ESPOUSING: *embracing*

It might have been otherwise, and, doubtless, was in the earlier years of the Norman rule; for the stalwart Saxon had been compelled to labor at the building of these mighty Norman keeps, and then, when they were finished, evil men took possession of them, and robbed and oppressed all who came within their reach. But there had been an end of most of these evil practices since Sir Valence had succeeded to his inheritance, for he was a sworn knight of chivalry, and by his vows he was pledged to defend the helpless and oppressed—not to wrong any man by false speech or robbery—and, unlike many of his brother knights, he believed his vow included the defense of even the downtrodden Saxon race as well as the honor of haughty Norman dames. So with as much honor and reverence as he would have wedded a Norman lady of his own rank, had he wooed and won Alftruda Ericson, the Saxon.

Many years had passed since she came, a shy, girlish bride, to live within the strong, gloomy-looking castle she had often shuddered at before, and sons and daughters had been born to them, who were taught all the arts and accomplishments deemed needful for Norman knights and ladies, with the usual scorn for the conquered race.

It was not often that the Lady de Valery indulged in such a reverie as then occupied her mind, for she generally banished all thought of her old

REPRISALS: *use of force to pay back for damage suffered*
MINSTER: *a large or important church*
STALWART: *strong, sturdy*
A REVERIE: *thoughts*

home and relatives as quickly as they arose; but now these thoughts would not be dispelled try as she would, and so she had given herself up to them until interrupted by the appearance of her bower-maiden.

"My lady, a messenger bearing a letter awaits thee in the great hall," said the maid.

"Send the messenger to me," commanded the lady in an imperious tone, "or bring the letter thyself."

"Nay, but the child will not give up the letter to any but the Lady de Valery herself; she is so commanded by—"

"Nay, trouble me not with such whimsies, but fetch the letter hither and I will read it anon," interrupted the lady.

To venture a further protest would probably bring a sharp blow from the lady's spindle, which hung at her side, and so the maid turned at once and descended the steep, winding stairs built in the thickness of the outer wall.

But in a few minutes she returned again with empty hands. "The girl will not part with the letter, my lady," she said.

"The messenger is a girl!" exclaimed her mistress, "and will not deliver her missive to thy keeping?"

"She saith it is of such moment that she should see the Lady de Valery herself, and that her—"

IMPERIOUS: *commanding, noble*
WHIMSIES: *silliness*
ANON: *soon*
MISSIVE: *letter*

"Lead her to the bower," commanded her mistress, "I will see her ere long;" and she turned once more to gaze at the distant farmhouse, and wonder why it was she could not divest herself of the unwelcome thoughts that would obtrude themselves upon her mind.

"Perhaps this messenger and her letter may drive away the strange foreboding that seems to be creeping over me!" exclaimed the lady after some little time; and she rose from her seat and descended to her bower, where her maids were busy with distaff and spindle, and where, as she expected, her visitor awaited her.

One glance, however, at the fair, childish face made the lady tremble and shiver with an undefined apprehension of coming evil; and before she took the letter she commanded her bowermaidens to withdraw, and as they silently obeyed she secured the heavy oaken door with its wooden latch, and drew the tapestry curtain before it. Then she stepped back and took the letter mechanically, her eyes still riveted on the girl's face. "From whence hast thou come, child?" she asked at length.

"From Jerusalem," answered the girl in a low, sweet voice, speaking in French with a better accent than the lady herself.

Lady de Valery started. "From Jerusalem!" she exclaimed. "And thy mother and grandfather, child?"

MOMENT: *importance*
DIVEST: *free*
OBTRUDE: *thrust*
DISTAFF: *a staff used in spinning wool or flax*

"They are dead," whispered the girl. "They died in the dreadful siege, before Saladin and his hosts of paynim soldiers took the holy city."

The lady seemed to breathe more freely, and she glanced at the unopened letter she still held in her hand. "Thy mother is dead!" she repeated, "and thy grandfather too! Did they bid thee bring this letter to me?"

"My mother bade me bring it to her sister, the Lady de Valery," answered the girl, looking full in the proud lady's face as she spoke.

"Hush, hush, child! be not rash in thy speech concerning this matter," said the lady quickly; and, to hide her confusion and gain time to arrange her thoughts, she retired to a distant window to read the letter.

But the reading of this seemed to add to her perplexity and before she read to the end she crushed it in her hand, and came back again to where the girl sat.

"Dost thou know aught concerning the contents of this missive?" she asked.

"Yes; the good brother who wrote it read it aloud to my mother as her head rested on my shoulder just before she died."

"Was the 'good brother' a monk?" asked the lady.

"A monk and a knight—one of the noble brethren of the Hospital of St. John," answered the girl.

PAYNIM: *pagan, especially Muslim*

This answer seemed to perplex and annoy the lady more than anything that had been said before. "I am ruined, disgraced!" she mentally exlaimed. "Every knight in England will know that I am a Saxon, and every proud Norman dame will take her seat at the tournament before me;" and Lady de Valery marched up and down the room, kicking the rushes and sweet herbs that were strewn upon the floor in every direction. For nearly half an hour she so paced, and then, casting her eyes upon the hour-glass that stood near, she suddenly stopped. "My children will be here very soon," she said. "I cannot give thee an answer concerning this letter now—not until Sir Valence hath seen it. Thou mayst come tomorrow," she added as the girl slowly rose from her seat. She lifted her soft blue eyes pleadingly to the lady's face, but she turned proudly away, and drawing aside the tapestry curtain said, as she pointed to the door, "Be careful and discreet in thy speech when thou comest again;" and then she returned to the window once more to watch for the return of her children from their ramble in the garden.

In a few minutes they came trooping in—two boys and three girls—almost too eager to pay the accustomed reverence on entering their mother's presence, for each was anxious to tell the wonderful news of the arrival of a holy palmer, who had come straight from the Holy Land, bringing with him news that made every Christian heart stand

PALMER: *a pilgrim who carries a palm branch as proof of having visited the Holy Land*

still with affright, for the holy city had been re-
taken by the Saracens after being a Christian kingdom eighty-eight years.

These were all the facts the young de Valerys
had heard, but the boys were eager with their
questions.

"My mother, will there be another Crusade, and
will Guy go to fight the evil paynim hosts?" they
asked.

The lady started, and turned pale at the suggestion. "Guy! Where is he?" she asked, looking
round the room, for this last suggestion concerning her eldest, her darling son, added to her previous perplexity, seemed to have confused her mind
entirely.

The children looked at each other, and then at
their mother's pale face.

"Has Guy come home from Lincoln?" asked Gilbert.

"Home! Nay, nay, thou knowest he is esquire to
Sir Hugh de Laney," replied the lady petulantly,
recalling her scattered senses.

"If there is another Crusade, and Sir Hugh
should lead his knights to the holy war, then Guy
would go too, would he not, my mother?"

But the lady could only shake her head. "The
saints preserve us from another Crusade!" she said
at length, and then, hastily dismissing her children, she sent one of her maids to inquire whether her husband had returned from the abbey of

SARACENS: *Arabs*
ESQUIRE: *an attendant to a knight*
PETULANTLY: *irritably*

Crowland, where he had been to consult with the prior about the enclosing of some lands. The girl soon came back, and Sir Valence with her, and as soon as the lady and knight were left alone, she began her story by telling him of the arrival of the palmer.

"Yes, I have heard the direful news, and already my men are furbishing their arms, as though Saladin were at the castle gates. But thou hast had another visitor today, Alftruda!" suddenly added the knight, pausing in his restless walk up and down the room.

"Yes, I have a letter brought by—by—" and there the lady hesitated.

"Brought by thy sister's child," said the knight somewhat sternly.

The lady looked up in his face. "How knowest thou she is my sister's child?" she asked.

But instead of replying to her question he asked, "What is this curse that is said to rest upon thy house—the curse of the Ericsons? I heard naught concerning it until today from the prior of Crowland."

"There is no curse now!" almost shrieked the lady; "it was but a Norman lie against a Saxon monk, and, to take the curse from his children, my father died close to the holy tomb."

"And thou hast known this, Alftruda, and kept the secret from me?" said Sir Valence in a grieved tone.

PRIOR: *head of the monastery*
DIREFUL: *terrible*
FURBISHING: *polishing*

The lady's proud head drooped beneath her husband's searching gaze; but at length, with an inward shiver, she said, "How could I tell thee, Valence, that our house was under the spell of the evil one; nathless, too, my father had redeemed it from the power of Satan by prayers and fastings and penances at the sacred sepulcher."

The knight looked pityingly on his wife as she said this. "Didst thou know aught concerning thy father's vow, Alftruda—did he tell thee of this before he went away?"

"He told me the story of the curse even as I have heard it since from the prior of Crowland, for this ancestor who brought the curse upon our race was a monk of Crowland, and spoke slightingly concerning the power of St. Guthlac, who had shown great favor to our family," said the lady.

"This recreant monk was also accused of witchcraft, as well as of teaching strange doctrines to all who came near him, saying the pope was only a proud, evil man, and that it was not lawful to pray to the saints and Virgin, besides many other heresies condemned by holy Church. Was this the accusation thou didst hear?"

The lady bowed her head. "But it was Norman against Saxon, and we know how cruelly—"

"Nay, but, Alftruda, thy father believed it or he would not have vowed to take the curse away; and now, alack! his vow hath been broken, for this child should have died within the walls of Jerusalem,

NATHLESS: *nevertheless*
PENANCES: *voluntary punishments for sins committed*
SEPULCHER: *tomb*

and not have returned to her kindred."

"Then she hath brought the curse back with her!" gasped the lady.

The knight looked pityingly on his wife's horror-stricken face. "I wish thou hadst told me this story before," he said gently, and then, by way of comfort, he added, "There will, doubtless, be another Crusade, Alftruda, and so the curse may yet be averted from our children."

RECREANT: *cowardly, unfaithful*
AVERTED: *turned away*

Chapter II

A Visitor

THE consultation over the letter brought to Lady de Valery was a long one, but it was decided at length that the request it contained must be complied with, and Elfreda, the little orphan of Jerusalem, received into their family. What position she should occupy would be a matter of after consideration, and one the lady herself would decide. At present she would be expected to wait upon her cousins, who were about her own age, thread embroidery needles for her aunt, or help the bower-maidens to polish the bright steel mirrors that adorned the walls of their mistress' room.

All this was explained to Elfreda when she came the next day, and the little girl bowed her head in silent acquiescence of the plan; but she refused obedience to one command the lady wished to impose upon her—she would not promise to forget her connection with her uncle and cousins at the low, thatched farmhouse close at hand, or deny her father's relatives, because they, too, were

ACQUIESCENCE: *agreement*

Saxon merchants of London. In all else she was willing to yield obedience, even to remaining silent about her parentage, and being born in the sacred city.

The palmer, however, who had traveled in the same company as Elfreda, was not so discreet in his speech as Lady de Valery wished, for while he was entertained in the great hall with wine and savory dishes sent specially from the upper table to him, he recounted to his nearest neighbors some of the scenes he had witnessed, especially enlarging upon that of the capture of the holy city, and how the paynim conqueror, Saladin, had burst into tears as the long line of orphans and widows issued from the gates of Jerusalem. "They were of right his prisoners, and might have been taken to the slave markets of Egypt or Bagdad," said the monk; "but with the mercy of a Christian knight rather than a paynim infidel, he set them all free, and I brought to England one little girl, who is of kin to the Lady de Valery."

Of course the story did not lose anything by being passed from lip to lip among the servants and retainers; and so, as soon as Elfreda appeared among them, she was known as the "Orphan of Jerusalem." Her cousins, of course, soon heard the story, but to them it seemed too marvelous to be true.

"She is only a girl with fair hair and blue eyes, like—like—who is Elfreda like, Adelais?" asked her brother.

INFIDEL: *unbeliever*
RETAINERS: *attendants*

But the young lady shook her head. "I have not looked at her much," she said, "only I know her hands are large—larger than mine." And she held out her slender, delicate hand in confirmation of the fact.

"I know who she is like—the Ericsons, the farmer who is so proud of being a Saxon that he still wears a long beard like a savage," said Gilbert.

"I don't know anything about long beards, or those sort of people," said his sister, with a look of disdain, "and I do not think Elfreda can be like them, as she is *our* cousin."

But Gilbert was in a mood to tease his sister just now. It was far more to his taste to do this than to learn to count his string of beads correctly—to know what prayer each bead represented, and was supposed to be *said*, as they dropped through his fingers, and so, while he idly toyed with this task set by his confessor, he went on teasing Adelais.

"I wish you would walk as far as the edge of the wood one day and look at those Ericsons. They were rich once, and kept servants and slaves too, but they have to work in the fields themselves now, so you will be sure to see some of them tending the swine or driving the plow."

"I have no wish to see swineherds or plowmen," replied his sister.

"But I want you to go, Adelais. I want you to look at them, and see if you do not think them like our mother."

CONFESSOR: *a priest who listens to the confession of sins committed and then grants forgiveness*

"Our mother!" repeated the young lady in angry scorn. "Thou sayest our mother, so beautiful and noble, is like a Saxon swineherd! I will tell her what thou sayest," and before Gilbert could stop her the angry girl had darted from the room, and was on her way down the winding stairs toward the terrace where her mother was walking. Almost breathless, with anger and her run together, Adelais rushed to her mother's side, and was at once reproved for her want of reverence.

"This hath occurred twice of late," said the Lady de Valery, reprovingly. But though somewhat checked, Adelais was too indignant to refrain from telling her mother what had occurred.

"Nay, Mother, it is Gilbert who should be reproved for want of reverence, for he saith thou art like a Saxon swineherd."

For a moment the contrast between the weather-tanned, elf-locked, unkempt swineherd and her own dainty self only provoked a smile on the lady's face, but as she looked down at her daughter this gradually faded, and a deathlike paleness came over her at the girl's next words.

"My mother, Gilbert called you a Saxon," which to the young lady's ideas was worse than being a swineherd.

But before Lady de Valery could make any reply, Gilbert himself appeared upon the scene.

"My lady mother, I would not dare to think of you as Saxon," said the boy, now quite as angry as his sister.

WANT: *lack*
ELF-LOCKED: *tangle-haired*

"Hush! hush! my children; follow me to the bower," said the lady, leading the way to the castle, and resolving to question both culprits as to the origin of this quarrel. She had no doubt in her own mind but that Elfreda was at the bottom of it, as in truth she was, though not in the way the lady supposed.

She breathed more freely when she heard the whole story, and found that her children had no suspicion of the truth. Indeed, Gilbert was most vehement in his denunciation of the race.

"My confessor saith they are, and ever have been, an obstinate and recreant people, disobeying the commands of the holy father, who is to be worshiped as the glorified saints, and refusing to give up the reading of the Scriptures, which was translated by their king, Alfred, and therefore must be full of errors, since it is not the work of a monk nor has it received the blessing of the pope."

The lady looked at her boy's hot, indignant face, and for one moment wished she could speak in defense of her people; but she had not the courage to do this, though she did say, "Be not too rash in condemning these people from the mouth of a Norman monk. Thou knowest how the old hate still rankles. But let us not forget that Saxon hands built Crowland minster before a Norman was seen in the land."

"Nay, but, my mother, the cloisters of the abbey are now scarcely finished, and the masons came

DENUNCIATION: *condemnation*
RANKLES: *causes resentment*
CLOISTERS: *covered walkways*

from beyond the seas—from our home in Normandy—to build the great stone church."

"But there was a church of timber before this was built; and what is now known as the Isle of Wultheof was the Isle of St. Guthlac, and—"

But there the lady suddenly stopped, fearing that for a Norman dame, who held herself aloof from everything Saxon, she had already betrayed too intimate a knowledge of the old minster that had been burned down.

The children were interested in their mother's story of a place they knew so well, and pressed her to tell them more; but the lady shook her head and bade them go and prepare their lessons, for, unlike many of their companions—their equals in station—the young de Valerys were learning the clerkly arts of reading and writing. After her children had departed the lady took up her embroidery, but the large red dragon she was depicting on the canvas grew very slowly under her fingers that day. There was a good deal of whispering and half-suppressed laughter from the alcove too, where the bower-maidens sat plying their spindles.

Elfreda had been summoned from among them to take her seat on a low stool near the embroidery frame, and here she sat still as a mouse, holding the needle she had threaded, and carefully noting the lady's care-worn, anxious face, for it was unmistakably care-worn in spite of its beauty.

STATION: *rank*

They were still sitting thus when the door suddenly opened and Sir Valence entered, and with him a lad about seventeen. "My son, my Guy, what hath brought thee from Lincoln town today?" exclaimed the lady, forgetting at once all her anxious, foreboding thoughts.

"I came in attendance upon my master, Sir Hugh, and to see thee, mother mine," said Guy, warmly returning his mother's embrace, and glancing at Elfreda as he spoke.

"He hath brought us news, too," said the knight, looking proudly at his son.

"Good news I trust, Valence," said the lady with a slight tremor in her voice.

"Now, my lady mother, thou hast not looked at my braveries, and this is the handsomest doublet and cloak in Lincoln," said Guy, in a jesting tone of complaint.

"She will not see it again for many a year, perhaps," put in Sir Valence, by way of breaking the news.

"Nay, but this paynim Saladin who hath wrested the Lord's inheritance from the holy hands of His people will soon be cut off, and then, having won knightly fame, I may break a lance in my lady mother's honor at the tournament thou shalt give in honor of my return." The lad spoke in a gay, eager tone, but the mother's heart almost stood still at his words.

BRAVERIES: *finery*
DOUBLET: *a close-fitting jacket*
WRESTED: *forcibly taken*
GAY: *light-hearted*

"Another Crusade," she gasped, "and my boy must be taken this time. O, Valence, will the curse never be removed!" and she sank down upon her seat again and covered her face with her hands.

Guy looked from his father to his mother, as if asking an explanation of the strange words.

"My mother," he said, "to fight the Lord's battle is not a curse. The holy father hath promised the remission of all sins, and a full escape from purgatory, to all who join this holy war. The friars are daily preaching in the marketplace, and the hearts of all men are stirred within them to avenge the cruel wrongs of those who have perished in the fall of Jerusalem."

"I know all thou wouldst say, my son; and since it is known that Prince Richard hath sworn to go to Palestine, half Europe will go crusading mad; while widows and orphans, and mothers robbed of their children, will watch in vain for their loved ones' return."

"Nay, my mother, not *robbed* of their children; but giving them up to the service of the Church to fight her battles, they will share the blessings of the conquerors."

"Nay, I want no share in such blessings," said the lady passionately. "I only ask that thou mayst return in peace and safety. When dost thou depart?"

"Nay, I know not when the great crusading army

REMISSION: *forgiveness*
PURGATORY: *a supposed place of punishment where the dead pay for their sins before going to heaven*

will be ready, but I journey hence with my master tomorrow, for he will cross the seas to visit his friends in France, and rouse them to follow his standard to the Holy Land."

The lady was overwhelmed with grief at the thought of her son's speedy departure, and in the indulgence of her own feelings she forgot her husband's share in the trial, and that Guy himself must keenly feel the sudden sundering of all home ties as well as those of friendship, and that the lad needed some hopeful words of encouragement to carry away with him, rather than the memory of such selfish sorrow.

Unnoticed and forgotten, Elfreda stole out of the room while the lady was in tears; but she lingered near the door, and when her cousin Guy came out she ventured to speak to him.

"My father died fighting on the walls of Jerusalem," she said simply, "and he used to say his battle cry was enough to make any man brave. Shall I tell it thee?" she asked.

Hardly knowing whether he was in a dream, from which he should presently awake to hear his master's voice calling him, Guy answered, "Yes."

"Christ and His salvation," said the girl solemnly, and before he could ask who she was, and how she came to be living in his father's castle, she had glided away, and he went down to the great hall repeating the words, "Christ and His salvation."

HENCE: *from here*
STANDARD: *banner*
SUNDERING: *cutting*

He was received with eager acclamation by his father's retainers, who had heard of his departure, and would fain have joined him if they could; and in listening to the blessing of one, and the charge of another, he could only ask, "Who is the little girl who hath come to dwell here?" when he bade his brothers and sisters a hasty farewell.

"Only Elfreda," answered Adelais. "O, Guy, will it be very long before the Crusade is over?"

"I shall be an esquire before thou dost return," said Gilbert.

"Then thou shalt bear my lance at the tournament my father hath promised to give in honor of my return," said Guy.

"And I shall be the queen of beauty, Guy," said Adelais.

"Thou wilt ever be that, my fair sister," gallantly answered the young esquire, and so with gay words upon their lips the brothers and sisters parted; but as Guy walked slowly over the drawbridge and looked up at the battlements, he slowly and thoughtfully repeated the words, "'Christ and His salvation.' They are grand words; I wonder where the soldier learned such a battle cry."

EAGER ACCLAMATION: *enthusiastic shouts*
FAIN: *gladly*

Chapter III

The Pilgrimage

IT was a busy scene upon which the morning sun looked down in the tiltyard of the castle about a week after Guy de Valery's departure. Sumpter mules were being laden with all kinds of baggage needful for a long journey, and men-at-arms were testing their short swords and crossbows as in preparation for an encounter with foes. To a stranger's eyes it would have seemed that these were making ready to join the great Crusade, or to journey through a hostile country, rather than the peaceful errand of going on pilgrimage to Canterbury.

It was the Lady de Valery's wish to undertake this perilous journey, for at the miracle-working shrine of the new saint, Thomas à Becket, all prayers were answered, and nothing would satisfy the anxious mother's heart but to journey thither on behalf of her beloved son. The thought that through her Guy was half a Saxon, was almost a comfort now, for surely the saint would look with

TILTYARD: *area for jousting*
SUMPTER: *pack*
COPE: *a long cloak worn by the clergy*

most favor on his own people—he who dared the
wrath of their king, to hold the rights and privileges of the Church and clergy with all the bold-
ness and daring of his English character—surely
he would protect her darling, who was as much
English as Norman.

Sir Valence loved his son, too, but he was not
at all willing to undertake this pilgrimage at first.
Prayers at the shrine of St. Wultheof or St. Guthlac
in their neighboring minster of Crowland would
be quite as well, he said, and with the additional
offerings of a cope and altar-cloth to St. Dunstan,
that this old English saint might not be offended,
surely her prayers would be answered, and Guy
would come back unscathed, laden with honors,
and the fame of being the bravest knight who had
fought in the holy war.

The times were very perilous, he said. The dis-
sensions in the royal family, and open rebellion
of Prince John against his father's authority, gave
encouragement to the turbulent nobles who were
seeking to throw off their feudal allegiance, and
raise themselves into petty kings over their own
domains. The almost limitless power over the conquered people which the first William had given
his knights when he portioned out the land among
them, was bearing its legitimate fruits, and, having subdued the people, these haughty nobles
were now trying to throw off all allegiance to the
king, and wage war at their own will against their

ALTAR-CLOTH: *an embroidered cloth for the church altar*
UNSCATHED: *unharmed*
PETTY KINGS: *little kings*

neighbors if they happened to be weaker, or there was any quarrel between them.

Sir Valence pleaded this, and that to go to Canterbury he should have to pass through the territory of some who were hostile to him; and even if they did not fall upon his train and make them prisoners, might take advantage of the slender garrison left at home, and by a sudden surprise carry off their children; such things had been done before. But for each difficulty as it was proposed Lady de Valery had a remedy. Their children should be sent for security to Crowland, and she would dispense with the attendance of all but two bower-maidens and a small company of men-at-arms; and the knight, finding his wife so fully bent on making this pilgrimage, at length reluctantly consented to his lady's wish, and preparations for the journey were commenced.

The king himself had set the fashion of visiting the shrine of the rebellious archbishop, and now pilgrims from all parts of the kingdom were daily wending their way to the crypt of Canterbury minster, to offer not only their prayers, but costly gifts of jewels and gold cups, as well as money, altar-cloths, and richly embroidered vestments for priests and bishops.

The Lady de Valery would not go empty-handed; and her servants who were to join in the sacred service likewise took offerings of their own,

SLENDER GARRISON: *small number of troops*
WENDING: *making*
CRYPT: *a chamber underneath a church used for burial*
FEN: *marsh*

so that two sumpter mules were laden with the gifts to be offered to St. Thomas à Becket. With these most carefully guarded against the attack of thieves, the cavalcade set forward one morning early in the spring of 1189.

The lady looked back as they crossed the draw-bridge, and then down into the dark waters of the moat, and with a prayer that her boy might soon cross that narrow bridge and mount those lofty battlements again, she rode forward close to her husband's side, and drew her veil down as if to hide all view of the obnoxious Saxon farmhouse near which their road lay.

The journey from the fen country to the chief city of England's garden—Kent—was a long one, and not free from danger, for where the road lay through a forest they were each moment liable to be attacked by one of the numerous bands of outlaws who, driven by the cruel oppression of the nobles and the forest laws to form themselves into robber hordes, made these forests their resort, and set at defiance the magistracy of the country.

But, to the great relief of Sir Valence, they came at length within sight of the towers of Canterbury without having had a single brush with either the robber bands or hostile nobles; and now that all danger was over, and the road almost crowded with pilgrims bent on the same pious errand as themselves, Lady de Valery proposed to alight

RESORT: *place of refuge*
SET AT DEFIANCE: *defy*
MAGISTRACY: *magistrates*
PIOUS ERRAND: *errand of devotion to God*

from her palfrey, and, putting off her sandals and the rich cloth pelisse she wore, walk barefoot and wrapped in a coarse serge cloak the remainder of the journey. But to this her husband objected. "Thou mayst kneel at his shrine, since the holy father hath seen good to make him a saint; but to me, as thou knowest, he will ever be Thomas à Becket, the proud, ambitious chancellor who rebelled against his king, who, though warned of the danger of raising one of this English nation to a position of trust and honor, would not heed the warning. Marry, he hath repented of his folly since, I trow," added the knight.

"Yes, right sorely hath he repented of the cruel deed done against holy Church and her brave servant, and in this he hath set an example to all his people which they do well to follow, and I trust, my lord, that thou, too, wilt."

"Walk barefoot to the proud chancellor's tomb? Never!" exclaimed Sir Valence. "I tell thee that in setting himself in opposition to the king and to the enactment known as the constitutions of Clarendon, which makes the clergy amenable to the laws of the land, and forbids their appeal to the pope except by the king's consent—I say that in his opposition to this, and in his acknowledging only the authority of the pope, he was guilty of treason and rebellion."

"Nay, nay, call not the blessed martyr a rebel,"

PALFREY: *a saddle horse other than a war horse*
PELISSE: *cloak*
SERGE: *wool*
MARRY: *an exclamation of surprise*

said the lady, lifting her hands in horror at what seemed her husband's impiety. "He was a brave, true martyr, who set himself only to defend the Church and the right of the holy father to act as, in truth he is, God's visible image. Think, my Valence, what it would be if the king and his proud nobles could work their will with the Church. I have heard thee say many times, that but for the power the Church has gained no home would be safe from the violence of lawless men; and that wives might be carried from their husbands, and children from their parents, if they were not protected by this same power, which even kings are forced to reverence."

"Yes, it is as thou sayest," acknowledged Sir Valence, with a sigh as he thought of the many evil deeds of which King Henry had been guilty— deeds, however, that à Becket, as either chancellor or archbishop, had never been known to reprove; but when the king sought to make the clergy amenable to the laws of justice, then the prelate could be bold enough in reproof.

"Then, if our king reverence this power for which St. Thomas died a blessed martyr, surely we, his people, do well to follow his example. Thou knowest, too, that a notable miracle was wrought in reward for the king's humiliation, for even while he was praying here at the shrine of the saint, William, the Lion of Scotland, was taken prisoner,

TROW: *believe or think*
AMENABLE: *answerable*
IMPIETY: *lack of respect for God*
PRELATE: *high church official*

fighting only a few minutes, for the blessed saint was fighting against him; and therefore would I beseech the saint with all humility to guard my boy in this dangerous Crusade."

"Willful women will ever take their own way, I trow," said the knight, and so the whole cavalcade halted, and Sir Valence had a tent pitched on the neighboring common, where his wife and her bower-maidens prepared themselves for this last stage of their pilgrimage.

The lady followed to the very letter the example set by the king, and partook of nothing all day but bread and water; and now, in the garb of a penitent, she set out with bare feet to walk the last mile of the rough road. They were swollen and bleeding before the city gates were reached, and each step cost her agonizing pain; but the daintily-reared lady kept bravely forward, refusing to moisten her parched lips with anything but water. Weak, faint, and exhausted, the shrine was at length reached, and, with a cry that was half-pain, half-joy, she threw herself on her knees, and at once began her supplication to the powerful saint. All night she kept her vigil by the tomb, and with prayers and tears besought a blessing for her son—a blessing that should crown him with honor and fame, and give him a long life, too.

And who shall say that God, in His infinite pity, did not hear the prayer thus ignorantly offered by one of His creatures, and did not comfort that

CAVALCADE: *procession of riders on horseback*
COMMON: *public field*
PENITENT: *a person sorrowing over his sins*

The Pilgrimage of Lady de Valery

anxious mother's heart, although she knew it not!

Sir Valence took little share in the devotions at the tomb of the saint, but he assisted his wife in presenting her votive offerings; and having given handsome presents to the abbot and prior of the monastery, where they had been lodged during their stay, he gladly turned his face homeward.

Lady de Valery could now talk of the coming Crusade, and listen to all the news which her husband could collect concerning the progress made in the gathering of men and treasure to be transported to Palestine, for was not her son under the special guardianship of the most powerful saint in heaven's hierarchy?

But it seemed that the new Crusade was likely to be forgotten for a time in the nearer interest of their own more immediate concerns, for nothing was talked of now but the alarming illness of their heart-broken king, who had been robbed of most of his continental possessions by his rebellious sons. The crowning agony of his life had just fallen upon him in the knowledge that his favorite, John, had joined his brothers and taken up arms against him, and men whispered among themselves that the old king would never survive this last blow, and what would happen if he died while Prince Richard was abroad.

The state of England was sufficiently deplorable now, despite all King Henry had done in reforming

VOTIVE OFFERINGS: *offerings of devotion*
CONTINENTAL POSSESSIONS: *lands and territory on the European continent*
DEPLORABLE: *wretched*

the civil administration of the realm, and introducing the first principles of trial by jury; but what it would become during an interregnum should one occur, when each powerful baron would struggle to place himself foremost, men trembled to think. Little wonder was it, then, that the shrine of à Becket was thronged with devotees, for the poor recognized in him the first man of their own nation who had been raised to any high position in the State since the Norman conquest, and above all, the martyr defender of that power that could alone stem the torrent of lawless violence in their haughty rulers. Even Lady de Valery felt a secret satisfaction that she could claim kinship with this man of the people when she saw the crowd of devotees at his shrine, and O, surely her darling would be safe under such a mighty protector!

So with a lightened heart and cheerful countenance she rode through the grassy glades of the forest, entering without fear the thick copses that might perchance prove the lurking place of some band of robbers, for her boy was protected by more than mortal care from all dangers, and for herself she feared nothing. In the depth of her gratitude to St. Thomas she now resolved that, in addition to the Fridays of each week, which the pope had commanded should be kept as Lent during the next five years, she and her bower-maidens would observe Wednesday also as a strict fast in memory of the martyr of Canterbury; and in

INTERREGNUM: *period with no king*
COPSES: *wooded areas*
LENT: *days of fasting and repentance*

forming these plans, and thinking of her son, the journey lost much of its wearisomeness, and they were once more drawing near their home when a sudden storm came on, which compelled them to look around for shelter. Seeing a swineherd near, Sir Valence directed one of his servants to fetch the man to him, for the rain was descending in torrents, and the lightning had already set their horses rearing and plunging, so that for his wife, at least, some shelter must speedily be found. Lady de Valery was almost as frightened as her palfrey, when a heavy clap of thunder rolled along the sky, and seemed to break over their very heads, so that she scarcely noticed the uncouth figure that was half-led, half-dragged before Sir Valence. He was dressed in a close, sleeveless jacket of sheepskin, from which the wool had only been partially removed, and which, fastened loosely round his throat, descended to his knees, and thus saved all necessity for any other garments. Around his neck was a brass ring, on which was engraven his name and the name of his master, which, if the Lady de Valery could have seen, she would have known was that of her brother. But no one noticed anything beyond the man's sullen, dogged look, which, with his matted, unkempt hair and beard, and weather-stained skin, made him look almost ferocious.

In answer to Sir Valence's question, the man silently pointed toward an opening in the woods they had not before noticed; whereat the knight, plac-

CLOSE: *tight*
DOGGED: *stubborn*

ing his wife on his own horse, and carefully leading the animal forward, bade his servants follow
him with the baggage as quickly as they could.

Sir Valance expected to find the dwelling of a
franklin near at hand, and did not notice, in his
anxiety for his wife's safety, that they were drawing near a larger dwelling than was usually occupied by those freemen—for they alone were free
from yielding feudal service for their holdings at
this time—and he had blown his horn loudly for
the gate in the stockade to be opened and the
drawbridge to be let down over the deep fosse that
encircled it before he noticed that it was the farmhouse hall of his wife's brother, Ericson. It was too
late now, however, to seek another shelter; so, his
own castle being still a mile or two farther on, as
soon as his summons had been answered, he took
his wife in his arms and carried her into the hall,
where the family were assembled.

Hasty as was their entrance, however, the knight
noticed at once that he had interrupted someone
reading from a clumsy-looking book that lay on
the upper table, while to the lady's ears had come
the words of the reader, sweet and clear, yet sound-
ing above the din of the elements without: "Let not
your heart be troubled."[1] The reader had stopped
there; and Lady de Valery recognized in the fair-
haired girl who had been performing this service
her sister's orphan child, Elfreda.

[1] JOHN 14:1
FRANKLIN: *a medieval English landowner of free birth*
FOSSE: *moat*

Chapter IV

William Longbeard

LADY DE VALERY had not thought it needful to send Elfreda to the convent with her own children, and the bower-maidens left behind had their own affairs to think of, so that the little girl was left to wander about at will. Sometimes she penetrated to the lower regions of the castle, where the under-servants, slaves, and dogs lived upon an almost equal footing; and sometimes she amused the grave old seneschal, as he kept watch and ward, with stories of travel and strange adventure, which she had heard from pilgrims and knights in her old home among the Jewish hills. To wander outside the precincts of the castle had been a forbidden pleasure while Lady de Valery was at home, but she had little difficulty in persuading the guard to lower the drawbridge now, that she might go forth in search of willow wands and wild flowers, and she was out in search of such floral treasures when the storm came on and drove her to seek shelter at the farmhouse, as it did Lady de

SENESCHAL: *the head of the household servants*
WATCH AND WARD: *guard*
PRECINCTS: *immediate surroundings*

Valery. This was explained by Ericson, who stood at the end of the long, low-roofed hall, wearing his beard as long as his father had worn his, and bearing himself as proudly as any Norman baron.

"Thou art welcome to the shelter of this Saxon roof, Lady de Valery," he concluded as her attendants began bustling in with the baggage. Her bower-maidens drew aside their robes in disgust as they were invited to sit down on an oaken settle near the massive table that was still strewn with the remnants of a feast, while the retainers and servants scowled at each other and muttered curses under their breath.

As this motley crowd came hurriedly into the great hall, Ericson descended from his seat on the dais and came forward a few steps to meet his sister; not that he intended to acknowledge the relationship between them. "Norman or Saxon is welcome to the shelter of my roof, and to all it will afford," he said, as he paused to escort the knight and lady to seats befitting their rank.

"We thank thee, courteous franklin," said the knight, as he took his wife's hand to lead her forward.

The bower-maidens, watching their mistress' face, did not wonder that she looked pale and agitated at being thus summarily introduced to a Saxon kennel, as they chose to consider it; and they were still more shocked when they saw Ericson lead her to a seat next his own at the upper

SETTLE: *a long wooden couch*
MOTLEY: *greatly varied*
DAIS: *a raised area at one end of a medieval hall where the head table stood*

end of the hall. It was the seat she had always occupied in the old days, when her father sat where her brother now did; and if the lady had not been so angry, and so fearful lest her secret should now be discovered by her domestics, these thoughts might have softened her heart toward Elfreda. But now all her care was to guard her secret; and so, while the confused hum of the servants talking among themselves rendered it safe for her to speak, she interrupted the formal conversation of her husband and brother by saying, "This Elfreda hath kinsmen among her father's people in the city of London, I trow."

"She hath," answered Ericson, shortly.

"Then if they will receive her for awhile—until —until my children be grown up, and she hath learned discretion, I will be at all charges for food and raiment." The lady glanced at her husband as she said this, expecting to see some sign of approval in his face; but Sir Valence looked as though he had not heard a word.

"Thou wilt approve of this—that Elfreda shall go to London at our charges," she said, a little anxiously.

"Elfreda is thy kinswoman, Alftruda," said the knight in a low tone. "If thou willest she shall go to London, send her at thy charge; it is thy affair, not one concerning me or my esquires;" and having rid himself of all concern in the matter he turned to look at the faded tapestry hung around the

SUMMARILY: *quickly*
DOMESTICS: *household servants*
RAIMENT: *clothing*

walls just where they sat, while his wife discussed the business concerning Elfreda's immediate removal to London with her brother. This was not a difficult matter to settle, for her father's relatives, though poor, would be quite willing to receive the little girl, he said, without gift or fee; but this the lady would not hear of. She should go richly dowered, only she must go at once, and no mention of her name was to be made again. She had left the hall before any of the servants had entered, and so there would be little difficulty about this; and the lady congratulated herself once more upon her escape from what seemed to her, imminent danger of disgrace.

As soon as the storm had abated, Sir Valence bade his servants bring the horses from the outhouse where they had been sheltered, and, with many thanks to the hospitable franklin for his courtesy, the whole cavalcade set forward toward the castle, whose gloomy keep or *donjon* could be seen plainly enough now that the sun once more shone out on mere and meadow. Sir Valence rode silently by his wife's side for a short distance, and then he said, "Hast thou acted wisely in sending this orphan girl from thee, Alftruda?"

"How could I do otherwise, unless—"

"Thy lineage should become known, thou wouldst say," interrupted Sir Valence, calmly; "and that thou fearest—"

"For my children's sake," interrupted the lady in

RICHLY DOWERED: *with a large gift of money*
ABATED: *ended*
MERE: *pond*

turn. "For myself I care not; but only think, Valence, of our Guy going forth to the holy war: would not thy proud Norman knights refuse to fight by his side if they knew his mother was a Saxon?" and the lady shivered at the thought of such contumely being put upon her darling.

"But for this child herself—hast thou no thought for her?" asked Sir Valence.

"She will be well cared for in London, and the dower she will take with her may help her people to pay some of the unjust taxes that are still levied upon the poor of my race, that the rich Normans may not be so heavily assessed."

The lady would identify herself with the downtrodden race when it suited her, carefully as she ignored them at other times. The knight smiled at what seemed his wife's inconsistency.

"But hast thou thought that the child's sudden disappearance will excite wonder and surprise in our household?" he inquired.

The lady was disconcerted by the question. She certainly had not once thought of this; but her brain, ever fertile in expedients, was not long at a loss in providing one for this occasion.

"Valence, for our children's sake, we must be careful to guard this secret," she said; "we were not here when Elfreda went forth, but we can send in search of her as though she were lost, and our servants will think she hath been carried off, as many maidens have been."

CONTUMELY: *humiliating contempt*
ASSESSED: *charged*
EXPEDIENTS: *plans*

"Thou wilt ever follow thine own willful way, Alftruda," said her husband with something of a sigh; and as they drew near the castle gates he added, "Thou must see to this search thyself. As I told thee when I read thy letter, I will never meddle in matters concerning thy kinsfolk, only be careful that thou bring not trouble—aye, the very curse of thy house—on thyself and the children through thy crooked dealings with this orphan of Jerusalem."

Sir Valence was not altogether free from the superstitious awe and reverence with which men viewed everything connected with the Holy Land; and this, no less than his knightly vows, made him extremely unwilling to do aught against the girl who had been left to their protection. Lady de Valery shared her husband's feelings to some extent, or she would not have consented to receive Elfreda into her household at all; but her selfish love for her own children overcame even this superstitious feeling, and she resolved to send her to London at all hazards. Once away from the castle there would be no fear of any indiscreet speeches betraying her connection with the degraded subject race; so Lady de Valery rode over the drawbridge to her castle-home feeling that the brooding shadow had passed from her life, and that Guy being secure in the protection of the mighty St. Thomas à Becket, she could once more be gay and happy, and prepare for the next tournament to be held at Lincoln, or the grander one her husband would give on Guy's return from the Holy Land.

When Lady de Valery was informed that Elfreda had left the castle and not returned, she sent out several retainers in search of her; but all the news they could glean of strangers being in the neighborhood was the report that a party of Robin Hood's men, from Sherwood Forest, had been seen lurking in the wood close by. And so it was settled that Robin Hood had carried off the girl to some of his haunts—perhaps to attend his wife Marian, whom he was said to keep as a great lady in the heart of the dense forest; and Gilbert amused himself and annoyed his sister by talking of what he would do, when he was a sworn knight, to rescue the little girl from her captors.

Beyond this boyish talk, and an occasional reference to her strange disappearance among the servants and retainers, Elfreda was soon all but forgotten by the dwellers in the lordly castle, for affairs of more interest than the disappearance of a friendless girl soon occupied the attention of all England.

The king's unnatural sons had succeeded in wresting several of their father's continental possessions from him, and now, in his old age, it preyed upon his mind so that he even cursed them for their wicked conduct, but he felt it so keenly that his health rapidly gave way, and before the close of this year, 1189, news came that King

Henry had died of fever at Chinon, and that Richard, his eldest surviving son, was on his way to London, to be crowned before setting out for the Holy Land.

The little world of Bourne, with its deep shady woods, and slow creeping streams winding through the sedgy fens, scarce felt the ripple of such changes as even the death of one king and the accession of another now made. There had been a time when, among the Saxon inhabitants, such news would awaken a faint hope that this change would give them the longed-for opportunity of throwing off the yoke of the oppressor, and at the sound of the curfew bell, when all lights and fires were extinguished, men would mutter dark hints of what they would do in the coming time when there should be no curfew to curtail their social gatherings or disperse their stealthy meetings; but that time had never come, and only a few, like Ericson, ever believed it would dawn for Saxon England again.

In the busy world of London, however, the death of King Henry might mean the death of commerce and handicraft, the imposing of grievous taxes, and the repeal of charters granted to them by the late king, which freed every man born in the city from the domination of any of the powerful barons.

These charters had been granted to other towns besides London, and were almost the first amelioration of the condition of the Saxon inhabitants.

SEDGY FENS: *marshes full of rushes*
CHARTERS: *legal documents*
AMELIORATION: *improvement*

By these a father could give his daughter in marriage to whom he pleased, without obtaining the consent of the lord suzerain, or paying him any fee on the occasion. He could also leave his property to his children, which he could not do before, because all he had—being a slave—belonged to his lord. The charter also conferred on the people the right of having some share in the choice of magistrates to govern them, as well as the exemption from certain tolls and taxes.

That Prince Richard might curtail some of these privileges granted by his father was only too probable, and so, when the news came of King Henry's death, there was a great gathering of the Saxon citizens, with their aldmen, or aldermen, in their council chamber, and foremost among these was one who was known throughout the city for his kindness and evenhanded justice.

Like Ericson of Bourne, he still wore a long beard, and the long cloak of his Saxon ancestors, and the nickname of William Longbeard, given him in derision by some haughty Norman, was one of the most honored in London.

Everyone listened to the words Longbeard spoke, and he counseled that all men should quietly pursue their business until the coming of Richard, for he, like William the Conqueror, would be crowned in the great abbey erected by the last Saxon king, St. Edward.

So the meeting had broken up, and men went

LORD SUZERAIN: *overlord*
ALDERMEN: *magistrates*

back to their homes to talk of the wisdom of William Longbeard, and how little he feared any change in their condition.

But William himself was not so confident as his friends supposed. As he sat on the oaken settle near the wide, open fireplace, and looked at his wife with the baby on her knee, and the gentle, fair-haired girl by her side, he sighed deeply as he said, "I almost wish myself in the quiet place thou art so often talking of, Elfreda —this Bourne—with its unchartered liberty and slavery."

The girl lifted her head. "Will the city lose its charters, thinkest thou," she asked, for she had learned how much the citizens owed to these.

Longbeard glanced at his wife, and saw how white her face had grown at the mere asking of this question, and so he said hastily, "Nay, nay, child, but thou knowest that a new king must have new counselors and new ways, and Prince Richard hath sworn to go to the Holy Land, and will want goodly treasure from our coffers, I trow, and so we must bethink ourselves that we provide this without tumult or law-breaking on the part of our citizens."

"Thy talking of moneys hath brought to my mind that an old Jew came to see thee whilst thou wert at the husting today," said his wife.

"A Jew! Thou must be mistaken. I am no luxurious Norman, spending more of my patrimony in

COFFERS: *treasure chests*
TUMULT: *commotion*
HUSTING: *city court*

one year than it will yield in two. I have no dealings with Jews," he added scornfully.

"Perhaps he would fain have dealings with thee," suggested his wife, laughing; "for that I was not mistaken thou mayest be sure, for no one but a Jew would wear the square yellow hat and serge gabardine commanded by law to be worn by them to distinguish them from all others."

"That is true," replied her husband, "but what said the man?"

"That he would fain have speech of thee, for he had heard of thy skill in interpreting Norman and Saxon laws, and thy justice in dealing with all questions brought before thee."

"The knave, to talk of justice—a Jew to talk of justice!" exclaimed Longbeard, and the very thought of it seemed so far-fetched and ridiculous that all else was forgotten in the laughter which rang through the room.

When this had subsided, however, Elfreda looked up from her embroidery and said, "Dost thou think the Jews were always the accursed usurers they now are?"

"Nay, I trouble not myself with such questions as that, Elfreda; thou shouldst have asked that of some learned monk dwelling near their ancient city, if it ever was theirs."

"Dost thou doubt even this, then?" asked the girl in wonder.

"Nay, I tell thee I have not thought of this matter,

PATRIMONY: *inheritance*
GABARDINE: *a loose outer garment*
USURERS: *money lenders*

but I know that a Jew's word can never be taken; and it is enough for me that the Church hath pronounced them accursed for lending money upon usury; though why she should not curse them who borrow it, is what I fail to understand."

Chapter V

The Coronation of King Richard

BEFORE William Longbeard left home the next morning he was summoned to see a visitor, who had chosen to come at this early hour that he might speak to him undisturbed. Descending to the little, roughly furnished hall, he saw a man bent with age, but who bowed still lower as he saw the Saxon approaching. He did not venture to draw near for fear of giving offense, and it was with fear and hesitation, and a visible tremor in his voice, that he said, "I crave thy pardon, noble Saxon, for thus daring to approach thee;" and then, for the first time, Longbeard noticed in the dim light of the entry that his visitor wore the russet gabardine and high, square, yellow cap of a Jew.

He drew back instantly, as if fearing to come in contact with one of such a degraded race; while the old man continued to bow and apologize in the most abject humility.

"The God of Israel will requite thee for the favor thou canst bestow upon the poor old Jew—

RUSSET: *reddish-brown*
ABJECT: *wretched*
REQUITE: *repay*

for he is poor—old Nathan is very poor," said the old man as he shook his head and sighed.

The Saxon's lips curled in scornful disdain as he looked down at the bowed figure before him. "What wouldst thou have of me, Nathan?" he asked sharply.

"That which will cost thee nothing, but will be of great service to my people," replied the old man, again bowing.

"Something to save a few zechins, I dare swear by the holy rood."

"We are poor, very poor," hastily interposed the Jew, "but we cannot make these Norman knights believe it; and now that King Henry is dead, and Prince Richard will come here to be crowned, before setting out for the land of my fathers—"

"Thy fathers!" scornfully interrupted the Saxon. "Keep thy talk, Nathan, to the matter of zechins, and defame not this land of Palestine by claiming it for *thy* fathers."

The Jew bowed obsequiously, and turned in silence to the reproof.

"I will set forth before thee mine errand this morning. My people would fain pleasure the new king that we may abide in peace in this city, and—"

"And rob honest citizens by thy extortions. I would that the king would take every Jew with him on this mad Crusade. But go on, Nathan, tell me thine errand," said Longbeard.

ZECHINS: *small gold coins*
ROOD: *cross*
INTERPOSED: *interrupted*

"My people would fain pleasure the king by a present—we are poor, very poor, and we cannot give much, but each will of our poverty give a little, and it hath been deemed wise that this should be taken by two of our elders and laid at the king's feet so soon as he hath received the crown. What saith William the Saxon, for it is well-known that he is skilled in Norman laws and Norman ways."

"Nay, of Norman laws I may know something, since I have studied them for the advantage of my people; but of Norman ways William the Saxon knoweth little beyond the hatred he beareth to all the fashions that are un-English, and come from beyond the seas. But once more to thine errand. Thou art wise to give a present to Prince Richard, soon to be King Richard; but see thou do this business warily, not pushing thyself before better men, either Norman or Saxon, even though their gifts be less. And let not any of thy people presume to come near the abbey Church of Thorney, otherwise the Westminster, on that day to see the gallant show, lest mischief come of it;" and having given his advice, Longbeard once more ascended the stairs, leaving his visitor still bowing and offering thanks and blessings.

As he left the house, however, he looked less pleased at the advice just given him. "God of Abraham, our father, how long are thy people to be treated as dogs by these uncircumcised Gentiles! How long shall we mourn for the land these

OBSEQUIOUSLY: *submissively*

Nazarenes and paynim infidels are rending themselves to obtain! How long shall these stranger
feet tread the courts of our temple while they say,
'Set not thy foot within our churches!' Even this
dog of dogs, William the Saxon, dareth to say to
Nathan the Jew, 'Go not within the walls of our
temple lest mischief befall thee!' Let mischief befall, for wherefore should a Jew give gifts and see
naught for the goodly zechins he hath yielded up?
And, above all, why should we not note the jewels
worn by those who owe us great treasure, or will
come to borrow of us ere long? I will go to this
church if Richard hath aught from the coffers of
old Nathan, and my daughter Sarah shall even go
with me." Saying which, the old man drew his gabardine closely round him, for the narrow streets
were now becoming thronged, and if, through
his inadvertence, the russet cloak should touch a
Christian garment, insult, perhaps blows, would
follow most surely.

Everywhere men were busy now in making preparations for Prince Richard's reception and coronation, and the old Jew hastened to the dirty quarter of the town where his people lived, for they,
too, would be busy at this time, and the old man
chuckled as he thought of the profit that would fall
to his share out of the gay doings that were about
to take place. Jeweled swords and costly armor,
rich silken garments and embroidered hangings,
besides gold and silver lamps, jewels, and money,

NAZARENES: *Christians; followers of Jesus "the Nazarene"*
RENDING: *tearing apart*
INADVERTENCE: *carelessness*

would be borrowed at this time to grace tournaments and banquets in honor of the coronation; and Nathan went home and opened his coffers in readiness, and counted out the zechins that were to be his share of the gift to King Richard.

London was soon full to overflowing, for not only Richard's immediate train of knights and nobles followed him from the continent, but a large number who had gone thither to gather arms and men for the Crusade followed their ardent young leader back to his capital to urge him, by their presence, to make every effort to gather as much treasure as possible for the equipment of the fleet that was to carry them to Palestine. The Emperor of Germany, Frederick Barbarossa, had already set out with a land force, and Richard, with his Norman nobles, were all impatience to join him with a fleet, but to gather all the treasure he needed some months must necessarily elapse.

Meanwhile the preparations for his coronation were pushed on with all haste; and when at length the day arrived, the great abbey church of which Norman and Saxon alike were proud was found to be too small to accommodate the numerous train of nobles; so that many of their esquires were left outside to join in the procession afterward.

These formed an additional guard round the church, and effectually kept all intruders from approaching too near the sacred edifice. A few Jews had ventured to come out, but they kept in the

ARDENT: *passionate*
EDIFICE: *a large or massive building*

rear of the crowd of citizens, who were, for the most part, very orderly.

The proceedings inside the church had almost terminated, and the first shout of, "Long live King Richard!" was faintly heard, when all at once these joyous sounds were drowned by the cry of, "The Jews! the Jews! hunt them out!" and forth from the portal of the church came two or three white-headed old men, their russet gowns torn almost to rags, and their hoary locks disheveled. With a frightened, bewildered gaze, they stood irresolute for one moment, and the crowd of esquires, thinking they meant to pollute the church again by their presence, closed round them, and took up the cry of those who had driven them out, and shouted, "Jews! Jews! hunt them! hunt them!" which the crowd beyond quickly translated into, "Kill them! kill them!" for the men-at-arms, as well as the train of esquires, had used their swords upon their defenseless victims, and those who had committed the unpardonable offense of entering the church soon fell, covered with wounds. Some of their own people, in the outskirts of the crowd, vainly attempted to come to their rescue; but this well-intentioned movement had only the effect of bringing down the anger of the populace, who, forgetting the original cause of offense, now turned upon them with the cry, "Long live King Richard, and death to every Jew!"

In vain the unfortunate people tried to escape.

PORTAL: *door*
HOARY: *white with age*
IRRESOLUTE: *undecided*

They were hunted through the streets, and followed to their homes, and there plundered and murdered. All the pent-up violence and lawlessness which the Church alone restrained and kept in check found its vent that day, for the right of sanctuary, which flying to a sacred edifice gave every other man, even a murderer, was withheld from Jews; and so they were left to the mercy of a turbulent, angry crowd, who hated them while they borrowed from them, and called them thieves and extortioners while they decked themselves in their jewels and silks. Many a debtor rid himself of a troublesome creditor that day in the name of King Richard, and many a jeweled sword that had lain in Jewish coffers was dyed with Jewish blood before night came on, and the tolling curfew put an end to the bloody riot.

In the quiet street of the city where Elfreda lived with her kinsman, William the Saxon, little of the din of the riot made itself heard; only a few frightened people hurried along the narrow roadway sometimes, and from the looks and words of these Elfreda gathered that something unusual had taken place. A few of the houses in this street could boast of the luxury of having a few panes of glass in the latticed windows, and at one of these sat Elfreda, watching every passenger, and hoping Longbeard would soon come home to allay his wife's fears on his account.

As she thus sat, a gaily dressed esquire, mounted

SANCTUARY: *protection*
PASSENGER: *traveler*
ALLAY: *calm*

on an elegantly caparisoned horse, and bearing a large bundle before him, suddenly appeared, and looked up with a bewildered gaze at the windows of the houses as he passed. As he came opposite Elfreda and looked at her, he reined in his horse and beckoned to her to come down to him, and in the same moment she recognized him as her Cousin Guy. Without a moment's hesitation she went down and unfastened the wooden lock of the door, and the next moment Guy carried his heavy bundle into the hall and laid it on the floor at her feet.

"Thou hast a gentle face," he said as he stooped down and began to unfasten the cloak that was wrapped around his burden, "and if thy father's heart may be judged by thy face, he will give shelter to this poor wretch even though he be a Jew, as he doubtless is. I have done what I could to save him;" and with a sigh, the young man uncovered the pale, blood-stained face of the old Jew who had come there a few days before to ask counsel of William Longbeard. Elfreda recognized him in a moment.

"Thy prisoner will, doubtless, be succored by William the Saxon, my kinsman," she said a little proudly, for she thought her Norman cousin would not acknowledge her here. But Guy had been too much occupied with the old man to notice Elfreda more than to see she was a maiden with a kindly face; and even now, as she spoke he stepped back

CAPARISONED: *decorated*
SUCCORED: *assisted*

Guy's Rescue of Old Nathan

a pace or two, and passed his hand before his eyes, and looked again before he said, "Art thou Elfreda, from my father's castle at Bourne?" and as he saw the smile part Elfreda's lips at the look of wonder on his own face, he bowed with courtly grace before her. "The saints have been favorable to me today," he said; "I had not thought to see a Bourne face in this riotous city of London. How sayest thou—this William the Saxon is thy kinsman? is he also called Longbeard by his fellow-aldermen and citizens?"

"Yes, he holdeth still to the fashion of our fathers in the cut of his beard," answered Elfreda, still smiling at her cousin's evident bewilderment.

"And thou sayest he is thy kinsman; and I have heard that thou art of kin to my mother, the Lady de Valery. Solve this riddle for me, gracious lady."

"Nay, nay, let this riddle be even as it is. This poor Jew claimeth our care now," she added.

The young esquire looked down with mingled pity and disdain. "I wish he were not a Jew, or not a man at all, that I could leave him to perish as a dog. Whither shall I bear him?" he asked once more, lifting his unwelcome burden.

Elfreda led the way to a small unused room in the rear of the house, and then went to fetch wine and restoratives. She had not helped her mother bind up her father's wounds in vain, and her knowledge of what should be applied was most useful just now, for Guy could do little beyond holding the bandages and supporting the patient while Elfreda poured a little wine down his throat. After a time he began to revive, and turned himself on the impromptu couch Guy had made for him of some loose straw and old sacks.

"Where am I?" asked the old man, feebly groaning forth the words.

"Fear not, thou art with friends," answered Elfreda; and then for the first time she wondered how it was her cousin came to have a wounded Jew in his care, for in his surprise at seeing her he had forgotten all explanations.

He told her in a few whispered words of the horrible riot that was still going on, and how he had barely escaped detection more than once while trying to save this man.

Before the recital was at an end Longbeard himself came home, and Elfreda fetched him at once to see the old Jew. He was looking anxious and perturbed, for this riot might bring upon them consequences little thought of at first. King Richard might make this the plausible pretext for withdrawing the charter, or imposing fresh taxes to pay the expenses of the new Crusade and the sight of the old Jew lying there wounded and helpless under his roof did not tend to lessen his perplexity. He glanced at Guy's dainty apparel with something of disdain, but he listened patiently to Elfreda's story of old Nathan's rescue, and when it was concluded he stepped up to Guy and held out his hand.

IMPROMPTU: *improvised*
FEALTY: *allegiance*

"It is our Saxon fashion of fealty and friendship; and thou art the first Norman whose hand hath been grasped by William the Saxon," he said as he clasped the white, delicate hand of the young esquire. The grasp was nonetheless warmly returned, however, and Guy said eagerly, "I trust I may know thee better by and by, for Elfreda hath a riddle to solve for me and—"

"This is no time for solving riddles, thou wouldst say," whispered Longbeard, "and I am of the like opinion; wherefore hasten back lest thou shouldst be missed from the banquet. I will take care of old Nathan, Jew though he be, since thou hast saved him. The saints preserve us! but what will not happen when a Norman saves a Jew and grasps the hand of a Saxon!"

Guy laughed as he slowly made his way back to the door, and after he had mounted his horse he called to Elfreda to say he should visit them soon to hear the solution of the riddle.

The friends of old Nathan were secretly informed that he was in safety; but they were afraid to venture beyond their own quarters in search of him, and William Longbeard was equally afraid to make it known where he was hiding. The king had suddenly announced that he had taken the Jews under his protection, and what this might portend no one could tell; only it was known he had little friendly feeling toward the citizens, and had been heard to say that he would sell London if he could find a cheapman who would buy it, even

PORTEND: *foretell*
CHEAPMAN: *merchant*

as he had already sold the earldom of Northumberland to the bishop of Durham for ten thousand pounds.

All sorts of such sales were taking place just now. Crown lands, houses, and offices of all kinds, were publicly sold to increase the money in the treasury, all of which would be taken to defray the expenses of the Crusade; while the unusual sight of a monk preaching might be daily witnessed now, crowds gathering to hear the exhortation, or rather papal command sent forth, that all men should join the holy war, and go forth to rescue the sacred city from the hands of the Saracens.

In the midst of all this public excitement, however, Guy found time to come again and again to the quiet home of William Longbeard, and by dint of questioning and talking he gradually drew from Elfreda all she knew of the family history, and the curse that was attached to the house of Ericson. He had been shocked, almost stunned, at first, on hearing that his mother was one of the despised Saxon race; but he grew alarmed when he heard of the curse that ever followed each member of this doomed family.

"And thou, Elfreda, and my gentle mother, are ye both under this curse?" asked Guy anxiously. He forgot his own share in it in his anxiety for them.

Elfreda bowed her head, and covered her face with her hands. "Nay, nay, do not talk of it, Guy;

PAPAL: *the pope's*
BY DINT OF: *by means of*

it makes me shiver and tremble as I think how—
how—"

"Nay, but tell me what thou wouldst say, Elfreda,
for I want to know all about this curse, and it may
be I can take it away, for thou knowest I am going
on this Crusade."

But the girl only shook her head. "It is of no
use, Guy; my father went crusading, too, and my
grandfather died near the holy tomb, and yet—
yet—O, Guy, I have brought back the curse to
England they say!" and Elfreda burst into such a
violent flood of tears that Guy grew quite
alarmed.

"Nay, nay, weep not Elfreda; thou hast not
brought this curse back. Listen to me; I am strong
and young, and can do valiant fighting against this
Saladin, and holy Church grants special favors to
those who are brave in battle. Now look up, Elfreda, and listen, and take courage. I am going to
fight for thee—to take this curse away—for when
honors and riches are offered I will put them from
me, and say, Nay, I want not these, but that holy
mother Church should remove the curse now resting upon the Ericsons."

Elfreda lifted her tearful face. "But O, Guy, if
thou shouldst fall in the battle!" she whispered.

"Nay, but thou shalt pray for me to our English
saint, Thomas à Becket, and I will be one of the
conquerors, and take the curse away, though others have failed."

And so Elfreda took courage from her brave young cousin's words, and began to hope that Guy de Valery would take the curse of the Ericsons away, although all others had failed in the endeavor to accomplish this result.

Chapter VI

At Crowland Abbey

IN spite of all King Richard's extraordinary exertions to augment his resources for the Crusade, it was not until April of the following year, 1190, that his fleet of a hundred vessels sailed from Dartmouth. Richard himself journeyed through France with a train of knights, and did not reach Messina until September, where he found his fleet awaiting him, and also received news that his mother would shortly join him with his promised bride, Berengaria, sister of the king of Navarre. His marriage shortly afterward with Berengaria, at Cyprus, gave great offense to his ally, Philip of France, and his waging war against Cyprus at the same time incensed Leopold, Duke of Austria. Philip was offended because Richard had been betrothed to his sister, Adelais, and Leopold because he had slain Isaac, king of Cyprus, his kinsman, and taken his daughter prisoner. But Richard could afford to laugh at his angry friends just now, for he was enjoying himself in his newly

AUGMENT: *increase*

conquered possessions, quite forgetful for the time of the terrible straits to which they were reduced in besieging the city of Acre.

For two years a Christian army had tried all the expedients of war, at a loss of three hundred thousand men, to regain this city from infidel hands; but Saladin would neither yield nor give up the holy cross which he had carried away from the Church of the Resurrection at Jerusalem.

Richard was at length roused from his life of pleasant ease at Cyprus, and, once aroused, he was not likely to be daunted by a few obstacles. The fever, which had carried off many brave men before a blow was struck, seized King Richard; but, against all warning, he mounted his horse day after day, and, though scarcely able to sustain the weight of his armor, he insisted on visiting the trenches, and cheering on the workmen who were erecting wooden galleries from which stones and darts might be hurled into the city, and where the bowmen and archers could do deadly execution among the garrison who mounted the walls.

Guy de Valery almost wished he were an archer himself, that he might by his bravery distinguish himself in the coming assault, and thus win from holy Church the removal of the curse under which the Ericsons had groaned for a hundred years; but there seemed little chance of winning this, or knightly fame either, for he was mostly employed as a messenger, going to and fro between the camp

STRAITS: *difficulties*
TREAT: *negotiate*

and the castle, where Queen Berengaria and her ladies resided. At length came the news that Saladin had proposed to treat for peace, and it was agreed that if they would give up Acre, and the still more precious cross they had stolen from Jerusalem, and set at liberty fifteen hundred captives, the allied sovereigns of Europe would withdraw their troops.

But, after forty days' delay, Saladin refused to accede to their terms, and then the hostages and captives, to the number of five thousand, were led out in the sight of the garrison of Acre and all slaughtered. It was almost the first of war's horrors that Guy de Valery had ever seen, and his heart sickened, and he hid his face for very shame at the thought of the cruel deed. Some of those thus basely butchered he had learned to know during their captivity, and, Turks though they were, he knew they were men with hopes, and fears, and warm heart-love for the dear ones they had left at home in Egypt and Arabia, just as he cherished the thought of mother, sisters, and friends in dear old England. He learned, too, that although they were called "infidels," and were supposed to worship only the false prophet, Mohammed, some of them, at least, acknowledged God to be their ruler and guide, and tried to live in obedience to His commands.

But not only Turks fell a sacrifice through this inhuman butchery, for Saladin quickly followed

ACCEDE: *agree*
BASELY: *dishonorably*
INHUMAN: *brutal*

the bad example set by these Christian warriors, and five thousand Christians were next murdered in sight of their friends and leaders; and then the *holy* war proceeded until the neighborhood of Jerusalem was reached, when famine and sickness compelled King Richard to beat a hasty retreat. Hearing at Jaffa that his old ally, Philip, who had returned to France, was conspiring with his brother John to deprive him of his throne, Richard was glad to make peace with Saladin on his agreeing to destroy Ascalon, yield up the coast of Palestine from Joppa to Tyre, and grant all Christians the liberty of going on pilgrimage to Jerusalem without tax or impost. Having concluded this compact, Richard and his distinguished army turned their faces homeward, the monarch sore perplexed how he himself was to reach the far-off shores of England; for Philip of France and Henry of Germany were both his sworn enemies, and, therefore, it was not safe for him to trust himself in their dominions; while Leopold of Austria was scarcely more friendly, for Richard had turned him out of Acre because he refused to take his share with his followers in laboring at the fortifications.

At length Richard decided to travel in the disguise of a pilgrim, hoping to reach England long before his fleet and army; but when at length these reached the shores of their native land, they found Prince John had made himself master of his brother's dominions, and nothing had been heard of

IMPOST: *tribute*
COMPACT: *agreement*

King Richard since his vessel had left them at Marseilles.

It was a sad homecoming for many a brave crusader, and mourning, rather than joy, was spread through the land as the news traveled from town to town that the army had returned from Palestine; but their king had mysteriously disappeared—for men had begun to look forward to the coming of their king to release them from the exactions and tyranny of Prince John.

Perhaps no one among Richard's knights and esquires felt more sad than Guy de Valery; for beyond the empty glory of having defeated Saladin, and performed prodigies of personal valor, Richard had accomplished but little for the Christian cause in Palestine, and Guy had no opportunity afforded him of winning that fame that he had fondly dreamed would secure from the pope the removal of the curse resting upon his mother's family.

Lady de Valery, however, thought of nothing, cared for nothing, now that her darling had returned in safety, and she begged that there might be jousts and tilting matches held in honor of his return, since Guy himself objected to the long-looked-for tournament.

"Art thou so disappointed at not having taken knightly vows, my son?" she asked one day, coming suddenly upon Guy as he leaned pensively over the battlements.

EXACTIONS: *forced payments of excessive sums of money*
PRODIGIES: *extraordinary, marvelous or unusual deeds*
PENSIVELY: *deep in thought; sadly*

The young man started at the question.

"I—I longed for knightly fame, my mother, that I might—" and there he stopped, for he recollected that he had promised Elfreda never to betray his knowledge of his mother's relationship to the Saxon franklin Ericson.

The lady thought she had discovered the cause of her son's hesitation, and she said with a faint smile, "So thou wouldst win knightly fame to break a lance in some fair lady's honor, who will perchance smile as sweetly on thy antagonist, and care little for thee and thy doughty deeds."

Guy tried to smile in response to his mother's bantering words, but the effort was a failure, for his thoughts went back to Elfreda, and the bitter curse that she was said to have brought back in her person; and so he only shook his head as he replied, "Nay, my lady mother, I have seen no maiden so fair as thou art, or whose colors I would choose to wear at tilting match or tournament. I seek not knightly fame for lady's favors," he added.

"Then wherefore art thou so sadly serious, my son? Wilt thou not tell me what is troubling thee? Gilbert is practicing with the men-at-arms in the tiltyard, and it is passing strange that thou shouldst choose to sit thus alone when our lithsmen are in such high revel at thy safe return."

"Gilbert and our men-at-arms can doubtless enjoy a mimic joust in the tiltyard, but, my mother, I

DOUGHTY: *valiant*
REVEL: *delight*

have been on the battlefield with King Richard—
have seen him fight hand to hand in no mimic
warfare, and would fain fight myself as our king
hath fought."

The lady sighed. "Our king is the boldest and
bravest knight in Europe, and doubtless thou
wouldst fain go in search of him, my son, but it
were ten times more mad than this Crusade to
begin such a search. St. Thomas hath heard my
prayer for thee, and brought thee back safely, and
now I would fain see thee join in the sports while
thou art here, for thou wilt presently return to Lincoln, and it may be many months ere thy mother's
heart is gladdened with a look at thy sunburned
face again."

"It may be as thou sayest, for if Sir Hugh de
Laney should journey to London, I shall doubtless
go with him," said Guy; and to please his mother
he went down at once to the tiltyard to take some
share in the thrusting and shouting. But he soon
grew tired of this play. His mind ran continually
upon the curse Elfreda had talked about, and at
length he resolved to set off to Crowland and ask
the prior for further information about this.

As he drew near the church, sounds of feasting
and merriment met his ears quite as loud, and far
less sober, than what he had left behind; and he
soon found that the monks, as well as the farmers and their laborers, were holding the "Feast of
Fools," and drinking scot-ale in the nave of the

FEAST OF FOOLS: *a medieval festival, normally held once a
year, mocking the officials and ceremonies of the Church*
NAVE: *main area*

sacred building in honor of the safe return of the crusaders.

The mirth and revelry grated on Guy's spirits just now, and he had almost resolved to reenter his boat and return home, when the prior met him and warmly welcomed him to the sacred isle.

"Thou wilt join our merry men in the feast," he said, leading the way toward the church.

But Guy held back. "Nay, I am in no mood for reveling, and if thou wert other than his reverence the prior of St. Waltheof's and Guthlac's, I should venture to say the saints would scarcely be pleased at their shrines being thus turned into tables for revelers."

The prior shrugged his shoulders. "The Church in her wisdom and compassion for the weakness of men hath accommodated herself to their love of pleasure and the good things of this life. But wherefore art thou so serious, Guy de Valery? Surely no ill hath happened to thy mother?" said the monk.

"As yet my lady mother is well, but thou knowest the curse of the Ericsons may at any moment fall upon her, and—"

"They have told thee this secret, then, though I charged Sir Valence to keep it safely locked in his own bosom. Foolish, foolish!" muttered the monk.

"No matter how I became possessed of the secret, it is enough that I know it, and that I have sworn to redeem my mother and all the Eric-

BLIGHTING: *destroying*

sons from the power of this curse," hastily added Guy.

The prior looked into his earnest face half-pityingly, half-scornfully.

"Thou art not the first who hath sworn such oath, and died with it unfulfilled. This curse spreads and widens in its blighting influence as it becomes known. I warned thy father when he wrung the secret from me never to let his children hear aught concerning it."

"But I have heard it," said Guy, "and I have come to thee to hear all thou canst tell me concerning it—all the records thy minster and monastery declare."

"Nay, we have no record of the chapters held by the brethren in olden time now, for they were burned with the old minster; but there is with us still an old man who can remember the talk of the older brethren when he came here a boy, and he likewise read the old records concerning the monk Leofwine, and the heresy he brought to this house from beyond the seas."

"Then I would fain see this old man ere it be too late, for if I know wherefore the curse came, I may know better what will tend to its removal. I pray thee, therefore, lead me to him!" he said, somewhat impatiently.

But the prior demurred at doing this.

"I can tell thee that it was through the shameful apostasy of a recreant monk; and our aged brother can tell thee little more than this, and that little is

DEMURRED: *objected*
APOSTASY: *abandoning of religious beliefs*

not reliable, for his mind is feeble now by reason of his great age."

Guy, however, would not be put off. "I must see this aged monk myself, and learn from his lips all he can tell me," he said.

"And then thou wilt go again to the land from which thou hast returned, for only at the holy sepulcher can such crimes as this be surely expiated."

"Be it so, then," answered Guy; "I will take upon me the vows of a Knight Hospitaler, and journey to Jerusalem, never more to return, if need be, so that this curse be removed."

Finding that he was not to be put off, the prior led him to the sunny side of the cloisters, where, remote from the noisy revel going on in the church, half a dozen aged monks sat talking and sunning themselves. To the eldest of this small party the prior led Guy, and introduced him as a young esquire who wanted to hear him repeat the story of the curse of the Ericsons.

The prior spoke carelessly, as though it were only a dead legend in which no one had an interest now; but the old monk shook his head gravely as he said, "Thou askest to hear a sorry tale, my lad—as sorry as it is true;" and yet the pleasure of having an attentive listener to his oft-told tale seemed to give the old man a sort of relish in the recital.

Carefully Guy noted every word, or rather every

EXPIATED: *paid for*

fact, for the old man was garrulous and discursive in his narrative, and Guy had to disentangle the main thread of the story from other minor details having but small connection with it; but as he retraced his steps homeward in the quiet twilight he carefully recalled the leading incidents, which were as follows:

About a hundred and forty years ago one Leofwine Ericson entered this house and became a monk. He was studious, and given to the study and use of herbs for medicinal purposes, and while here was accused of witchcraft. Then he went beyond the seas in search of a brother and the pursuit of knowledge, and was absent many years, during which he spent much time in Rome. Then the brother came back, not wild and lawless as he had once been, but paying little heed to the commands of holy Church, which thing was not much noted until the monk came back to this house, when he at once began to practice the outlandish fashion of preaching and exhorting the brethren, and all who would listen to him. But even this was not the worst, for in his sermons he boldly declared that the pope was a proud, evil, ambitious man, and that the only true faith was to be found among some people dwelling in certain valleys of the Alps, and it was well-known that these people had long declared themselves the enemies of the pope, and refused to worship the Virgin mother as well as the saints, and impiously declared that

GARRULOUS: *talkative*
DISCURSIVE: *rambling*
IMPIOUSLY: *disrespectfully*

the bread and wine in the holy Eucharist were not changed into the body, blood, and divinity of the Lord Christ, as the Church expressly declared. The old charge of witchcraft and the practice of magic was brought against him, for he was more skillful in curing the ailments of those who came to the monastery infirmary than any of the brethren, and likewise incited the people to hold fast by their Saxon Scriptures after it had been forbidden by the holy father. All these crimes would probably have brought swift destruction upon the offender, had not the hatred of Norman rule and Norman prelates made the monks slow to betray one of their brethren, and so this Leofwine was suffered to live and die in peace; but when it reached the ears of a later abbot he laid this curse upon all the Ericsons, as it was reported, whether truly or not, that the heresy had tainted the entire family; and that curse had never been removed.

EUCHARIST: *Communion*
INCITED: *encouraged*
SUFFERED: *allowed*

Chapter VII

The Curse of the Ericsons

AS Guy walked homeward he sifted out from the tangled mass of the story three distinct charges against the old monk—disobedience, heresy, and rebellion: rebellion, not against the State, but against that higher, greater power, the Church, which he thought enhanced the crime. Little wonder was it, then, that all bearing his name had been doomed to groan under a heavy curse ever since, and that evil and misery followed them wherever they went; and yet his mother and that gentle girl, Elfreda, what had they done to merit such a doom? Was it just of the Church not to remove this ban from innocent victims like them?

How much more bold and daring these questionings might have grown no one could tell; but at this moment Guy was aroused from the reverie into which he had fallen by the sudden reappearance of a party of his followers who had been sent to search for him.

"The Lady de Valery is sorely troubled at thy

ENHANCED: *magnified*

long absence," said the leader, as he reined in his horse close to Guy.

"Her care is needless, I am able to protect myself," answered Guy in a tone of annoyance; "how fares it with my hawk now? She was not able to mount upon my wrist when I came forth."

"Nay, I know not, for I am not skilled in the ways of hawks; but, doubtless, the falconer hath given all due care to thy favorite's ailment. Thou must hasten thy steps or the curfew bell will sound ere we reach the drawbridge," added the old retainer, placing himself at Guy's side, while the rest of the party fell behind.

He had scarcely done this when, drawing near a thick copse, a party of men sprang out upon them, roughly dressed in Lincoln green doublets, and each armed with a stout club, which they flourished around the heads of the retainers as soon as they offered any resistance.

"Deliver thy pouches," said the leader in a commanding tone; "we ease all men of such burdens;" and Guy was instantly dragged from his horse, while his captor drew forth a short sword and held it menacingly to his breast.

Guy laughed at the man's threat. "Thou must even take my pouch, but I warn thee that thou wilt find little in it, for Guy de Valery brought but little from the Holy Land, and is not at liberty to gain much here in poor England."

The man held back as he heard the name. "De

Valery," he said: "I have sworn that my hand shall never be lifted against a de Valery, though they be of the cursed Norman stock that eat up our land like grasshoppers. Ho, there, my merry-men!" he cried; "the clerks of St. Nicholas are not so fond of marks and zechins that they can forget their plighted words:" and before Guy could recover from his astonishment the band of outlaws had hastily retreated, leaving the young esquire and his party little the worse for the encounter.

"The accursed churls have more sense of honor than belted knights, in some cases," grumbled the leader, as though he repented the departure of their assailants. The men, however, who were but slightly armed and unequal in numbers, were evidently glad to be let off so easily, and Guy needed no further urging to hasten his steps homeward.

That their lord had by some unknown means won the favor of a powerful band of outlaws became the topic of conversation among his followers for the next few days, and Sir Valence himself laughed when Guy recounted to him the strange termination of the encounter.

"Better friends than foes," he said lightly.

But Lady de Valery looked very uneasy.

"Those Saxon churls are strange men," she said; "and though they doubtless have a good reason for showing favor to those of our name, I trow we were better without such doubtful distinction."

"Thou wouldst rather they had carried me off

PLIGHTED WORDS: *solemn pledges*
CHURLS: *rude, ill-bred people; from "ceorl" meaning peasant*

to their fastness in the greenwood until my father could ransom me?" said Guy, with a spice of mischief in his tone.

"Nay, I would rather thou hadst been here, or tending the flying of the falcons," said the lady. "But why didst thou go to Crowland?" she inquired of her son.

"There was a merry feast of fools in the minster, and free drinking of scot-ale, and all the village—"

"Nay; but, my son, thou art not given to feasting like these gluttonous Saxons and their swineherds," interrupted the lady.

"My mother, is it well to despise these Saxons as though they were dogs? As old Bracy said of these robbers, they have as deep a sense of honor as belted knight or sworn Hospitaler. My mother, wouldst thou be glad to see me a Knight of St. John, a Knight Hospitaler?" he suddenly asked.

"Nay, nay, Guy; thou hast been to the Holy Land, and let that suffice thee," said his mother, a little impatiently; "and as for espousing the cause of Saxon churls, it were better not to talk of this beyond thy mother's bower, for Prince John is said to hate them as bitterly as doth the queen mother, and will gradually withdraw from them all the liberties and immunities granted by his father."

"Then trouble will come of it; for these English, or Saxons, as they are sneeringly called—are a brave people, and I have heard that our great

FASTNESS: *stronghold*

conqueror, William, would have been driven back to Normandy if their chosen king, Harold, had not been slain in the first battle, for he was England's heart, and the nation was prostrated with grief at the loss of her hero, especially as there was no recognized leader to take his place."

"Guy, Guy, what art thou saying? who hath bewitched thee into loving this despised race?" and Lady de Valery trembled with fear lest her son had discovered his own near relationship to them. No one but herself knew how her days had become a bitterness and her nights a continual dread through this very thing, and now she almost shuddered as Guy lifted his large liquid eyes and looked so searchingly into hers.

If he had seen anything like encouragement in her face he would have poured out all his heart before her—told her of the secret he had become possessed of, and his determination to lift the curse from the Ericsons; but the lady had summoned all her pride of bearing to aid her in this critical moment, and Guy saw nothing in his mother's face but a cold, proud, haughty contempt for the despised Saxons; and a chill feeling, such as he had never known before, crept into his heart.

After sitting thus for a few minutes he rose from his lowly seat among the rushes at his mother's side and silently withdrew, and Lady de Valery covered her face with her hands and almost groaned aloud.

PROSTRATED: *laid out*

A few days later Guy returned to his duties at Lincoln, and to prepare for his master's departure to London. The lengthened absence of the king was causing the greatest uneasiness among his faithful followers; while his brother John, aided by Philip of France, was taking every advantage of his absence to oppress his subjects, so Sir Hugh de Laney and a few other knights had resolved to make some effort to discover the fate of their royal master. At present there had been no tidings of him received, and Sir Hugh laughed at the wild, romantic plan that had been proposed by one of the king's companions—a troubadour minstrel— which was to go through Europe with his harp and sing under the walls of every castle the songs Richard had often sung in the old days with him. Knowing the king's love of the old Provençal minstrelsy, his friend thought he would be sure to raise his voice in unison with the familiar strain; and the queen mother, who herself knew the power of song, hoped much from the troubadour's pilgrimage.

To grave old knights like Sir Hugh, however, the plan seemed so wild that it only provoked their anger to talk of it. There were whispers of the queen mother being crazy concerning everything that came from her Provençal home, and her love of the gay, luxurious southern Provençe, where she had been used to sit as presiding queen in the courts of love and beauty, held by these same troubadour minstrels.

According to all Guy heard, these poets were

TROUBADOUR: *wandering, traveling*
PROVENÇAL: *a dialect used in southern France*

as bold in defying the Church and denouncing the vices of the clergy as this poet was in braving the dangers of a search for King Richard, and he wished he could go to Provençe and hear some of their bold songs. Could it be worse to defy the Church by preaching than by singing, and if it were not, why had not the pope put down this troubadour minstrelsy?

Guy had not been long in London before he again went to see Elfreda, to make inquiries about the old Jew he had rescued. He wished he could have told her that the curse was removed from her family; but, alas! this seemed as far off as ever now, and Guy could only hope she had forgotten it during his absence.

He found Longbeard was more busy than ever now, giving not only his time, but as much as he could possibly spare of his means, for the relief and defense of the poor English citizens who were so heavily taxed to support Prince John's extravagance, and pay the debts of the Crusade.

Longbeard welcomed Guy frankly, but at the same time warned him that it might bring trouble upon him if it were known that he visited one so obnoxious to the Norman nobles.

"I care not," answered Guy, his eyes following Elfreda as she crossed the room. He wondered what the indefinable change could be that seemed to have come over her during his absence. He had left her little more than a child, and now she seemed to be transformed into a beautiful woman

MINSTRELSY: *minstrels' songs*

—as beautiful and stately as Lady de Valery herself, only Elfreda's face was calm and gentle instead of proud and haughty, like his mother's. Guy, too, felt shy and nervous in her presence, and dared not say what he had intended; and yet he came again and again, and talked of the Crusade, and the king's matchless prowess, and Saladin's chivalry. But it was a long time before Guy could venture to tell her of his visit to Crowland, and what he had heard there. The idea of a curse being connected with that calm, gentle, helpful woman, who was evidently the sunshine of her household, and the dearest friend of both Longbeard and his wife, seemed as wild and unlikely to Guy as the troubadour's search for the king seemed to his anxious nobles.

Guy was sent now and then as a messenger to Normandy, where King Richard's wife and mother were living, and at length he returned with the startling news that the king's prison had been discovered at last; discovered, too, by the troubadour who had been scorned and sneered at so much. The minstrel had journeyed through France, Germany, and Austria, singing close to each castle that came in his way. At last his patient perseverance had been rewarded. At the Castle of Tiernstein, where he sang a lay composed by himself and the king conjointly, the stanza of Richard's composition had been sung by a prisoner inside the walls

PROWESS: *exceptional bravery or skill*
CHIVALRY: *knightly, noble actions*
LAY: *song*
CONJOINTLY: *together*

in response to his own refrain; and that this prisoner was the captive king, he felt sure.

The tale seemed hardly credible to the matter-of-fact citizens of London, but it was soon confirmed by the news that Duke Leopold of Austria had sold their brave king to the emperor of Germany for ten thousand pounds. Loud and angry were the protests of clergy and people, both Norman and Saxon, at this ignominious treatment of the champion of the cross, and a petition was at once sent to the pope praying him to excommunicate both the duke and emperor for their conduct in the matter.

The archbishop of Canterbury, Longchamp, thought it better, however, to appeal to the emperor, and to learn through him the terms on which the valiant though indiscreet king of England might be restored to liberty. By his influence it was arranged that the unfortunate Richard should appear before the diet at Haguenau to clear himself of the charges brought against him, and his defense so moved the diet that his chains were at once ordered to be removed, and a treaty arranged for his ransom.

It was joyful tidings for the citizens of London, who were groaning under the exactions of Prince John, and hoped much from the known generosity of King Richard; but when it was made known that a hundred thousand marks must be raised as the

CREDIBLE: *believable*
IGNOMINIOUS: *humiliating, disgraceful*
EXCOMMUNICATE: *banish from the Church*
DIET: *an assembly of the princes of the Holy Roman Empire*

price of his ransom, the heavily-taxed people almost despaired of ever seeing their king again, for how could this vast sum of money be got together from their impoverished country!

Longbeard grew more anxious too, for he knew that the downtrodden Saxons of the city, so unequally taxed as compared with their richer Norman neighbors, were now talking of revolt, thinking that the absence of the king, and the unpopularity of Prince John, would be a good opportunity for the election of one of the old line of Saxon kings. Had there been the least chance of success Longbeard would doubtless have favored the plan; but he knew that every town and village in England was frowned upon by a Norman fortress, whose lord could easily put down the insurrection of the few franklins and their servants who lived near. He knew, too, what his more ignorant countrymen failed to perceive, that this Norman conquest had not been an unmitigated curse to the land, cruel and harsh as their rulers were. No! no! the Normans had brought with them the arts of a civilization almost unknown in Saxon England, and a temperance and chivalry undreamed of before: and though drunkenness and gluttony might still prevail, the Norman chivalrous treatment of women, and their higher refinement and respect to law, were exerting a widespread and deep influence for good upon the English character and manners, and softening much of their

INSURRECTION: *uprising*
UNMITIGATED: *unbroken*

former ruggedness and ferocity.

To the far-seeing Longbeard a blending of the opposing races was the only hope for England; but how this was to be effected while England remained but a feudatory part of Normandy, and her kings were forever striving to grasp the crown of France, and thus reduce her to a petty province, he could not see; but he was content to wait, and steadily opposed all the schemes of the would-be rebels. He cheerfully contributed his quota for the ransom of King Richard, and helped many of the poorer citizens to do the same; but with all the people's willingness to give, it was some months before the required sum was collected; and it was not until the following year, 1194, that King Richard reached England. To the great disappointment of his subjects, he made only a short stay when he did come, and then hastened once more across the channel to make war against King Philip for his perfidy in helping his brother to usurp the kingdom, caring very little that London was still groaning under the exactions which had been imposed by the usurper.

FEUDATORY: *tributary*
PERFIDY: *treachery*
USURPER: *someone who takes something they have no right to*

Chapter VIII

The Challenge

THE war with France continued for two years with varying success, most of the money needful for its prosecution being drawn from England, while the murmurs of the Saxon citizens of London grew louder and more ominous. Longbeard was their declared leader now, and he appeared for them before the municipal council, declaring that the taxes were unfairly levied, and threatening to appeal to the king if this was not remedied. His threat was laughed at, but Longbeard was not a man to be ridiculed out of a purpose, so he crossed the sea, and went to Richard's camp and boldly stated his grievance.

The king promised to investigate the matter, and Longbeard returned quite elated to London; but, alas! his joy was of short duration. That a Saxon should dare to seek an audience of the king was something so unheard of that the Norman rage knew no bounds, and the first thing he saw as he entered the postern of London Bridge was the

POSTERN: *gate*
QUITTING: *leaving*
PRIMATE: *bishop*

proclamation of the chief-justice forbidding any commoner of London quitting the city without permission under the penalty of being imprisoned as a traitor. Confident of the king's promised protection, Longbeard advised that should the calls of business require any tradesman to leave the city, he should do so without regard to the proclamation. Many, however, shrank from doing this, for Hubert Gautier was not only chief-justice, but primate of England, and therefore disobedience to his commands as archbishop was rebellion against the Church.

Stamford Fair, however, proved too strong a temptation for even this fear. Many tradesmen wanted to go, some of whom went without obtaining the required permission, and were arrested and thrown into prison.

No word had come from King Richard, and Longbeard, despairing now of the promised redress, placed himself at the head of his countrymen, who formed themselves into an association for mutual defense, and collected all the arms they could get together—staves shod with iron, hatchets, and iron crowbars. Fifty thousand desperate men thus armed was no insignificant force, and Longbeard, for the first time, seemed to lose his prudence when he saw this multitude gathered round him. To show his contempt for Norman usages and rule, he commenced his harangue by quoting a text from the

REDRESS: *righting of wrongs*
USAGES: *ways*
HARANGUE: *long, passionate speech*

proscribed Saxon Scriptures, which at once gained for him the ear of the people, for they had clung with the utmost obstinacy to the use of the vernacular Scriptures, to the great annoyance of their Norman prelates. Had Longbeard been more prudent and less confident something might have been gained by this popular rising; but after the primate had convoked several meetings of the citizens, and addressed them in his office of archbishop, promising them full redress of all wrongs, and punishment for sedition, the number of Longbeard's followers began to decrease. They dared not disobey the Church, and the wily archbishop, seeing the power he had gained over them, next claimed, as chief-justice and regent, a child from every family of Saxon descent, to be held in Norman fortresses as hostages for the preservation of peace. The citizens were taken by surprise, but they yielded to the demand.

Guy de Valery had just returned with his master from Richard's camp, and incautiously went to see Elfreda and inquire about her safety the very day this demand was made known.

He was still at the house when Longbeard returned from a consultation with his fellow-aldermen concerning his approaching trial before the archbishop. Spies and friends alike had accompanied him home, the latter assuring him he had nothing to fear, an assurance Longbeard seemed scarcely to need while he was with them,

PROSCRIBED: *banned*
VERNACULAR: *common language*
CONVOKED: *called*

for he was himself sanguine as to the result until he came into his wife's presence, and his eyes fell upon their only child, who sat on the floor at her feet. Then all his firmness forsook him, and covering his face with his hands, he turned toward the window, that none might see the agony depicted there.

In a moment Guy was by his side, frankly holding forth his hand. "We are kin, Longbeard," he said, "and I will carry thy wife and child to a place of safety. I will set off this very night to Bourne if thou wilt give them to my charge."

The Saxon turned his white, haggard face and looked pityingly at Guy. "Thou sayest truly, we are kin, and thou art foolish to come here. I warned thee of thy danger before, and told thee, too, the Church forbade thy union with Elfreda," said William.

A heightened color stole into Guy's face as he answered, "It was not of Elfreda alone I was thinking, but of thy child. Suffer me to carry her to my father's castle for safety, and thou canst say she is in a Norman fortress for safekeeping."

"And thinkest thou that thy father's castle will be deemed fortress enough for Saxon children? Nay, nay, not even for his own will this suffice. The few drops of Norman blood flowing in thy veins will not save thee from insult if it is known thou art kin to William the Saxon."

"It is known," gasped Guy, pale with horror at the

SEDITION: *rebellion*
REGENT: *one ruling in place of the king*
SANGUINE: *confident*

thought of what might befall his family through his want of caution.

"Hasten, then, to Bourne with all speed, for thy father is known to favor the Saxons under his rule, and if it be known he is connected with William Longbeard, his Norman blood will count for little in these evil days."

"But Elfreda and thy child! Let me take them with me," pleaded Guy.

"Nay, they will be safer in London at present," replied Longbeard. "I have seen old Nathan, the Jew, and he hath promised to take care of them, and, if need be, to bear them across the sea, where I also purpose to join them by and by."

"Nay, but were it not better to cross the sea with them thyself at once," urged Guy, and in this plea he was seconded by Longbeard's wife, as well as Elfreda.

But the sturdy patriot tore himself away from the tearful caresses of both wife and child. "Wilt thou with these lamentations break my heart, and make me forget I am an Englishman?" he inquired somewhat sternly. Then, turning to Guy, he said, "Thy duty is plain: hasten to Bourne, and give thy father timely warning of the danger impending."

"And thy duty is—"

"Hush!" interrupted Longbeard in a commanding tone. "My duty is to stand by my countrymen in this hour of peril, and deliver them from the tyranny of Church and State."

In vain Elfreda and Guy pleaded that the care of his own family was now of paramount importance, and that little could be hoped for when the enemy held their children as hostages.

Longbeard was immovable in his determination. "I have sworn," said he, "to be the friend of the poor, as Norman knights swear the oath of chivalry, and I will not go back from my word;" and as he spoke he glanced at Guy, who had so recently taken that oath on the battlefield in France.

"It is enough," he said. "There is English chivalry as well as Norman. Thou art right, Longbeard, and henceforth I am an English knight."

At nightfall Guy sallied forth, fully armed, but with only one esquire, to give warning to his friends at Bourne what they might expect from any messenger coming from London. He traveled with all the speed the bad state of the roads would allow, never drawing rein until within sight of his old home, except to change horses; but the journey was a long one, and when faint and almost exhausted Guy at length reached the drawbridge, and blew the horn, calling for admittance, he saw, to his dismay, that other visitors had arrived there only a short time before him, and he guessed only too truly that they were messengers from the archbishop.

Silently and sadly the old warder lowered the drawbridge and admitted the newly-made knight, who should have been received amid the bray of

PARAMOUNT: *greatest*
SALLIED FORTH: *set out*

trumpets and the joyful shouts of all the men-at-arms. Very different was this homecoming of Guy's from what everybody at Bourne had planned.

The shouts, however, were not wanting when the younger men saw him, but Guy raised his hand in a moment, and commanded silence.

"Thou hast received other visitors today?" he said, glancing at the strangers' horses.

"Hubert of Grantham hath sent messengers from the lord archbishop," replied the old warder.

"Hubert of Grantham—my father's old enemy," exclaimed Guy; and, flinging himself from his horse, he made his way as quickly as he could toward the great hall, where his father was holding a parley with the unwelcome visitors.

"Say but the word, Sir Guy, and these messengers shall go to the bottom of the moat instead of Grantham," whispered one as Guy passed on toward the hall. He tried to appear calm and indifferent, as if unaware of the object of their visit, hoping that his fears might be groundless after all; but the first words that fell upon his ear dissipated these hopes.

"A son and a daughter of Sir Valence de Valery we are commanded to bear back with us to Grantham," said one.

"Nay, but I dispute the right," interrupted Guy, stepping boldly forward. "Thy pardon and thy blessing, my father," he said, more humbly, "and thy forgiveness, too, for thus taking up this

PARLEY: *discussion*
DISSIPATED: *dispelled*

question; but I am belted knight, even as Sir Hubert of Grantham, and I have sworn to suffer no wrong upon any man which my good sword can redress."

"Nay, nay, thou knowest not whereof thou art speaking, my son," said Sir Valence with a slight tremor in his voice as he glanced at the parchment lying open before him, and which seemed to be the men's warrant for their demand. Guy looked at it, too, and saw that the whole family were classed as Saxons, wholly ignoring the Norman descent of Sir Valence himself. The knight had been too much absorbed in amazement and horror at the demand made to notice this or aught else, but that a son and daughter must be given up to the care of his cruelest foe; but Guy saw this at once. He had not looked over legal documents with Longbeard without catching some of his acumen in detecting their plans.

"We are not Saxons," he exclaimed, "and this demand is illegal."

"Be not hasty, my son," said Sir Valence, and he leaned forward and whispered a few words in his ear.

But instead of looking shocked and disgusted, as the old knight expected, Guy answered: "I know it all, my father, but I am still an English knight, and I claim the right of an Englishman to defend the oppressed. See to it, ye Normans, and bear the gauntlet of Guy de Valery to Hubert of

ACUMEN: *ability*
GAUNTLET: *glove; in this case, sent as a challenge to a duel*

Grantham, for thou shalt not touch either brother or sister on that warrant," and as he spoke Guy drew off his glove and threw it down before the messengers.

They looked up in blank surprise at the daring young knight, while a shout from the de Valery attendants echoed through the castle reaching even to the room of Lady de Valery.

"Thou darest our master to single combat!" exclaimed one of the messengers, picking up the gauntlet.

"I challenge him to meet me in the lists whensoever and wheresoever he will," replied Guy defiantly; and, once more speaking a few words of apology, he left the hall and went up to his mother's bower.

Lady de Valery had been told of the coming of the messengers and the object of their visit, and now she was sitting among the rushes upon the floor almost speechless with despair and humiliation. She turned her head as Guy entered the room, and, seeing who it was, started to her feet, and rushed into the arms of her son.

"O, Guy, my son, thou hast won thy knightly spurs fairly and honorably, but thy knighthood is of little worth now!" she exclaimed.

"Of little worth!" repeated Guy, "and wherefore not, my holy mother?"

"Because—because—O, Guy, thou hast not heard of our dire disgrace, that thou art not of

LISTS: *an enclosed area for combat*

pure Norman descent, and therefore our children
are to be taken from us."

Guy turned aside his head for a moment to conquer his emotion, and then, speaking as calmly as
he could, he said: "My mother, I have long known
this family secret, and have, I fear, helped to bring
this trouble upon thee;" and then he went on to
tell her of his acquaintance with Elfreda and her
Saxon relative, Longbeard, who was the leader of
the late insurrection.

Lady de Valery shivered as she listened to his
story. "O, the curse, the curse! that girl hath truly
brought it back upon us; even as they said she
would. If it had not been for her none need have
known that thy mother was a Saxon;" and the lady
sank down among the rushes again, as if utterly
crushed by the weight of her misery.

Bitter as his mother's sorrow was, however, he
could not bear to hear Elfreda blamed, and so
gently raising her to a chair, he said, "Nay, nay,
my mother, blame not this girl; for if thou hadst
kept her with thee this thing might not have been
known—or, at least, not thought of just now. For
myself, however, I care not, for I have learned to
glory in the name of Englishman, and mean to
be known as one of the bravest knights of English
chivalry. And now, my mother, listen to me. I have
learned something from this William Longbeard,
the Saxon—learned to know a legal from an illegal
demand, and this that hath been sent by Hubert

of Grantham is an illegal one, for it demandeth two children instead of one, therefore the messengers must e'en depart without either, to get this amended."

"Nay, nay, Guy, deceive me not with such vain words, but let me seek strength from the saints to part with my children if need be," said the lady sadly.

"The saints will help thee, my mother, when the time comes; but we feed not our hawks until they be hungry, and so the saints will not help thee tonight for a trial that may not come for a month. Listen to that shout! The messengers have even now departed."

"Gone, and I have not bidden farewell to my children!" exclaimed the lady, starting forward.

But at this moment the arras was pushed aside, and her husband entered the room. "Calm thyself, Alftruda, and thank the saints that Guy came home tonight, for the messengers have departed, carrying only his gauntlet to Hubert, their master."

"And my children are safe—saved by thee, my Guy?" and once more the lady threw herself into her son's arms. "But what sayest thou the messengers have taken?" she asked in a minute or two. "Surely, thou hast not sent a defiance to this Hubert of Grantham?"

"And wherefore not, my mother? Have I not fought under Richard the Lion-hearted, and thinkest thou my heart will turn to water at the sight of

E'EN: *even*
ARRAS: *tapestry*

a sword or battle-ax at a tournament? For this Hubert, in his vanity, will call all England together to witness his victory, I doubt not, and I shall be challenged to meet him thus in the lists."

"And it will be no child's play," said Sir Valence, with something of a sigh.

"I am beyond child's play now, my father. I am a man, and a sworn knight as well as a warrior, and I will meet this Hubert wherever he willeth."

A week later the summons came again from Sir Hubert to deliver up one child to his custody, and for the knight, Sir Guy de Valery, to meet him in open combat in the lists at Grantham.

Chapter IX

The Tournament

NEWS of the approaching tournament at Grantham, in which Guy de Valery was to play so conspicuous a part, was soon known throughout the neighborhood, and for a time became the all-absorbing topic. Saxon swineherds and slaves of all conditions, as well as Norman knights and proud ladies, were always anxious to be present at such a spectacle, and this about to take place had increased interest for the inhabitants of Bourne, for Guy de Valery was already known as a brave knight, and tender and gentle withal. Perhaps the fact of his being half-Saxon by birth had something to do with the lessening of the prejudice against him on the part of the oppressed race, for this was known far more generally than Lady de Valery supposed, and now it was openly talked of; in addition to which the trouble of the family at the castle in having to give up their son, drew them nearer to the hearts of their dependents.

WITHAL: *as well*

It was, perhaps, the first tournament Lady de Valery had not looked forward to with pleasure; and now, if it had not been that she was intensely anxious to be near Guy, she would gladly have remained at home or spent the time while he was fighting at the tomb of St. Waltheof, at Crowland, for she shrank from appearing in the pavilion among those proud Norman dames who would scorn her for her Saxon birth. The dreadful secret must be known throughout the length and breadth of England now, for it was this that had been the main cause of this tournament being given—their foe would triumph in their shame to the very utmost by publishing the cause of the quarrel about to be decided by combat. Guy, too, seemed obstinately bent on perpetuating the disgrace by refusing to appear as a Norman knight, declaring he would enter the lists as an Englishman, and the champion of English chivalry.

Lady de Valery alternately blamed Elfreda and that old monk of the Ericson family who had brought the curse upon them, but never once glanced at the possibility of being herself the cause of all this exposure and trouble. Her husband ventured to say that it would have been better to have kept the orphan girl with them; but the lady shook her head. "The curse would have been more dire in its effects if she had been here; see what hath befallen her kinsman in London: he is

PERPETUATING: *continuing*

charged with sedition, and his life may yet be forfeit through this curse."

In vain her husband tried to show her that Elfreda had very little to do with the public actions of Longbeard; she would not be convinced of that any more than she would acknowledge that it was her own pride that had brought this trouble upon themselves.

"O the curse, the curse!" she wailed, as she sat rocking herself on the floor, and for some days she refused even to direct her bower-maidens in their work, or select the dresses she and Adelais would wear at the tournament. Her soul was bowed with grief for her youngest darling who had just been taken from her and committed to the care of Sir Hubert; she was likewise full of anxiety for the fate of Guy—not that she doubted his bravery, but Sir Hubert was a tried and skilled warrior, and moreover, everyone would shout for him, while Guy would be left without a companion to enter the lists by his side. She was still bowed with grief when Adelais suddenly entered the bower looking very angry and indignant.

"Guy hath forgotten his knighthood, my mother; forgotten that he is even a Christian," said the young lady.

"Why, what hath he done now?" sighed the lady, wearily.

"He hath brought home a Jew! a Jew, my mother! one of the accursed race whom no Christian will approach."

But instead of being shocked, Lady de Valery started to her feet exclaiming, "Where is he—this Jew—he may be able to help us in our sore trouble?"

Adelais looked at her mother, fearing this sorrow had turned her brain. "My mother, if St. Dunstan and St. Thomas à Becket cannot help us, this old Jew cannot," she said.

But Lady de Valery had heard more about the power and learning of these, and their knowledge of the occult sciences and healing art than Adelais, and so she insisted upon going down at once to the entrance hall, where, on a low stool, apart from all the servants, who feared the contamination of his presence too much to go near him, sat an old man, white-haired and bent, dressed in a ragged gabardine.

He rose and bowed his head almost to the ground as the lady drew near, for in her anxiety to consult him, Lady de Valery forgot her pride—forgot everything but her anxiety to save her children.

"Old man, I have heard that thy people are learned in magical arts, and the knowledge of herbs and healing balsams, and I need the exercise of thy skill at this time."

The old man had grown pale while she was speaking, and now trembled like an aspen leaf as he said, "Father Abraham, help me. I came not hither, gracious lady, to practice magical arts, but a goodly knight found me fainting by the way, and brought me hither to rest and refresh myself. Old Nathan is poor, very poor; he hath been despoiled of his goods until he hath but this coat and girdle left. I cannot give thee gold or jewels to release me, but—"

"Nay, nay; I want not thy gold, old man, but thy skill for this same young knight who brought thee hither. He is to fight in the tournament at Grantham, and he—he may be sorely wounded,"—and the lady's voice quivered as she spoke.

The Jew looked at her curiously, as raising his eyes to her face he said, "My people hath learned somewhat of this healing art, but I am poor, very poor, and the balsams and medicaments to cure wounds are costly, and I have not a silver penny in my pouch."

"Nay, I ask thee not to spend thy money, old man, I will give thee what thou needest for the purchase of herbs and balsams, and for the other matter—" The lady drew a step nearer and spoke in a lower tone, and the shivering fear returned upon the old Jew as he listened.

"The God of my fathers deliver me! Dost thou think I can restore thy child by magic? Nay, nay, I tell thee the old Jew knoweth nothing of this witch-craft, for God hath forbidden His chosen people to pollute themselves."

But the idea of a Jew fearing contamination appeared so ridiculous to the lady that she turned away in contemptuous scorn. But she stopped

DESPOILED: *plundered*

again when half across the hall. "Thou art jour-
neying to Grantham, I trow; see to it that these
balsams are in readiness should they be needed,"
and she threw a handful of small coins toward the
old man.

He gathered them up eagerly and put them into
his pouch, chuckling as he shook them together,
while Lady de Valery returned to her bower to
make more active preparations for the journey
and tournament.

It was not long, however, before Adelais came
in again with the news that her brother was bringing another visitor to the castle, and this time she
drew her mother to the window to watch the approach of the curious cavalcade now drawing near
the castle gates.

By the side of Guy rode a tall, sun-browned man,
dressed in a scarlet cloak, cut somewhat after the
fashion of those worn by monks, and adorned with
a white cross on the shoulder. A cap of the same
color, turned up with meniver, was on his head,
but as the cloak was blown on one side as they
halted at the drawbridge, the underdress became
plainly visible—a shirt of linked mail, with sleeves
and gloves of the same, so close and so finely woven that it might have been of silk but for the glit-
ter of its tiny steel links.

"My mother, who can this be? Hath the old Jew
departed?" asked Adelais; but she did not heed
her mother's answer, for she was watching the

MENIVER: *light-colored fur*

stranger's war horse, which was led behind him fully accoutered, with the headpiece and spike projecting in front, while at the saddle hung his master's battle-ax, richly inlaid, his plumed headpiece, and two-handed sword. All the appointments were so rich and costly that Adelais felt sure that their visitor was no less a personage than King Richard or Prince John, and was somewhat disappointed when her mother said:

"Our visitor is a Knight Templar. One whom Guy hath doubtless met in Palestine, and who, having but just returned, hath heard nothing of our shame and disgrace."

"My mother, if this great knight would but go with us to the tournament we should not be so ashamed. Will Guy ask him, think you?"

"Nay, I know not what foolish thing Guy may not do now he hath changed his wardrobe, and chooses an ensign half-Saxon and half-Norman in color and device."

"Nay, but it would not be foolish to ask this knight to bear us company," said Adelais, who saw that it would add much to their importance to have him join their company, and take away the sting of having all those critical Norman eyes leveled at them alone.

The news that a Knight Templar was staying in the neighborhood brought the prior of Crowland to the castle; and hearing that he had come on purpose to accompany the young English knight

ACCOUTERED: *outfitted for battle*
ENSIGN: *banner*

into the lists, the worldly-wise prelate at once expressed a wish to journey with them, for the clergy were by no means averse to taking their share of whatever merry-making might be going on; and in spite of conventual rules and monastic poverty they were as fond of dress and display as Adelais de Valery herself. True, the fashion of his garments were strictly of the monkish shape, but the cloth was of the finest, and the sleeves turned up with the richest furs; the mantle secured with a golden clasp, while his well-fed mule was highly decorated and adorned with silver bells.

All these accessories of wealth and power being added to their train had wonderfully soothed Lady de Valery; and though she still looked forward with some anxiety to the result of the conflict, the thought of the despised old Jew who brought up the rear of their party, mounted on a sumpter mule, gave her renewed hope; for even if Guy was worsted and wounded in the encounter, the wonderful balsam and herbs old Nathan was to procure from some of his people on the way would be sure to cure him quickly.

The gates of Grantham were reached at last, and here our party lodged for a few days to rest and refresh themselves after their tedious journey. It was evident now that Guy looked upon this coming encounter as no light matter, for just before setting out with his esquire, to take his place in the lists, he sought the prior of Crowland. "Shrive me,

AVERSE: *opposed*
MANTLE: *sleeveless cloak*
SHRIVE ME: *hear my confession*

my father," he said, humbly falling on his knees before the monk. "I would that I had come to thee before, for in the hurry of this time I may forget some sins I ought to confess."

"Nay, thou hast not been undutiful to Holy Church, who, as a merciful mother, forgiveth the sins of all her children," said the churchman lightly.

But the assurance did not seem to satisfy Guy just now. "What saith Holy Church about the forgiveness of sins—that only those confessed can be forgiven—is it not so?"

"Certainly, my son; hasten therefore to make thy confession," said the prior a little impatiently, for he was anxious to set out for the lists.

But it seemed that Guy could not think of anything he ought to confess, and yet he was dimly conscious of being burdened, weighed down, with an accumulation of unconfessed, and therefore unforgiven, sins, for which he must obtain absolution before entering upon the deadly conflict.

"Nay, father, I have been remiss in many of my confessions; sometimes hurried for want of time, sometimes forgetful of much that has happened. I cannot even now remember much that I ought to say, much that needs forgiveness; will not the Church in her mercy pardon—"

"Nay, nay, my son, waste not time in useless questionings. I have told thee what is the voice of the Church in this matter; hasten, therefore, to make thy confession."

ABSOLUTION: *formal forgiveness of sin*
REMISS: *careless*

So Guy detailed all he could think of as being needful of absolution, and the prior hurriedly pronounced the benediction; but Guy was not satisfied. If he fell in this encounter with Sir Hubert, how many years would he be doomed to purgatory for his unconfessed, unforgiven sins? and how much of this punishment would be remitted in consideration of his having fought in the holy Crusade for the rescue of Jerusalem? These were the queries that floated through Guy's mind.

It was a puzzling thought, and one that troubled Guy this morning; but he had little time to indulge in such serious reflections, for a blast of trumpets summoned him to mount his horse, and, with his esquire behind him bearing his lance, with its new ensign fluttering in the breeze, he rode forward, laughing gaily with his companion, the Knight Templar, who seemed determined to keep up his friend's spirits.

The place chosen for the tournament was a large meadow, enclosed by woods on two sides, and sloping downward to a level bottom, which was enclosed by strong palisades for the lists. A gate at either end admitted the combatants; and around the palisades were tents and pavilions, each adorned with the ensign of a knight, and occupied by his friends and family. Near the southern end sat Lady de Valery with Adelais, and a few ladies of similar rank; but Sir Hubert's pavilion, which was directly opposite, was

PALISADES: *fences made of stakes pounded into the ground*

crowded with the rank and fashion of the Norman nobility.

The Knight Templar had been eagerly welcomed to take part in the sports which were to occupy the greater part of the time, and his pavilion occupied a central position, and was given up mostly to the use of strangers. The townsfolk and yeomen found places on the slope of the hill, or even on the branches of the trees, for all were eager to see the mimic conflict. But none were so eager or impatient for the heralds to appear and proclaim the laws of the tournament as Lady de Valery; and when at length the signal was given for them to appear, she leaned forward white and breathless, wondering whether Guy would be first called upon to answer his challenge to Sir Hubert, or whether the sports would precede the more serious business of this tourney.

In a long preamble the herald stated the whole matter concerning Guy de Valery's challenge, and Adelais, as she heard it, drooped her proud head, and would fain have hidden herself from the scornful glances that she felt sure were being directed toward her; but Lady de Valery had gone through this part of the ordeal so often in thought, that, now it had actually come, she felt very little discomposure. Moreover, she felt relieved to hear that the challengers who were to fight all comers would be allowed to try their skill before Sir Hubert and Guy engaged in their combat.

YEOMEN: *farmers*
PREAMBLE: *introduction*
DISCOMPOSURE: *agitation*

Very calmly and indifferently did she watch the fall of knights, the killing of horses, and wounding of their masters, for it was to her but a pageant—a dull show—while Guy was waiting to be announced as the next to enter the lists. At length this mimic warfare came to an end. Splintered lances were removed out of the way; the musicians, who had urged on the combatants with martial strains of music, were allowed a few minutes to breathe, and there was a general flutter and clatter in all the pavilions and galleries, which was as speedily hushed, however, on the herald, prefacing his notice with a flourish of trumpets, announced the names and degrees of the contending knights, Hubert de Grantham and Guy de Valery.

When the two opponents stood facing each other at opposite ends of the lists there was but one opinion in that crowd of eager faces. Guy de Valery could never stand the shock of an encounter with the gigantic Hubert. His father himself grew pale as he compared the two, while Lady de Valery hid her face for a moment to call upon the saints for aid in the unequal conflict.

As the trumpets gave the signal for attack the knights flew from their posts like lightning, meeting in the center of the lists, and shivering their lances, while their horses were thrown back upon their haunches.

Lady de Valery screamed, "My son, my Guy, he is down! he will be trampled to death!" but the

MARTIAL: *warlike*
PREFACING: *introducing*

next moment she saw that he had righted himself in the saddle, and was waiting for Sir Hubert to rise, for he had rolled off his horse, and lay on the ground apparently senseless. Guy rode back to his post again, and received a fresh lance from the attendants; but still Sir Hubert did not move, and someone stepped forward and removed his helmet to give him air.

There was a moment of breathless suspense as the attendant bent over his prostrate master. The next minute it was known that he was dead—had died as he fell from his horse, and the conflict was at an end.

SENSELESS: *unconscious*

Chapter X

The Old Jew

GUY sat gazing vacantly at the scene of commotion in the middle of the lists, his lance still in his hand, as though he were waiting for another opponent to spring forward. No one noticed him now until a faint shriek from Lady de Valery attracted the attention of a few bystanders, and then they saw that the young knight had fallen from his horse, and now lay as helpless and prostrate as Sir Hubert himself.

"'Tis witchcraft," whispered one.

"Nay, nay; but the saints have taken up the quarrel of Sir Hubert, and struck this presumptuous young knight, who calls himself the champion of English chivalry," said a townsman.

"English chivalry!" sneered another. "But 'tis well he did not present himself in the lists as a Norman, or he would have been flouted with his Saxon birth."

"'Tis well, perhaps, that St. Dunstan and the other saints have taken this quarrel into their own

FLOUTED: *mocked*

hands, for the lithsmen of Sir Hubert would he less merciful, I trow."

"Nay, nay; St. Dunstan hath had no hand in smiting down one of his own nation. If this De Valery, of Bourne, hath been struck by other powers than witchcraft, 'tis by other saints than the English."

Lady de Valery heard every word that was spoken, but she took little heed of either the speakers or their words until Guy was carried into the pavilion and the old Jew summoned to attend him.

His armor was removed by the practiced hand of the Hospitaler, and it was soon seen that nothing more mysterious than a deep wound from Sir Hubert's lance had caused the temporary faintness and loss of blood. Everybody praised Lady de Valery's forethought in enlisting the Jew's services. The Knight Hospitaler walked outside the tent as the old man entered, while the rest of the company, although of less sanctity than the sacred knight, removed themselves to a distance from the Jew's contaminating presence—all but Lady de Valery; she forgot everything but that Guy lay wounded before her.

Sir Valence had gone to the pavilion of Sir Hubert to make further inquiries into the cause of his death, and perform the last ceremonies needful for the settlement of this quarrel, and learn, if possible, something concerning his younger son, now in Sir Hubert's hands. But it seemed that he had not succeeded in his errand, for, before the old Jew

SANCTITY: *holiness*

had finished dressing Guy's wound, he came back, looking very anxious and perturbed. Without noticing his wife he stepped up to the old man, and asked how soon Guy could be removed—whether it would be safe for him to commence the journey at once.

"Thou wouldst take him back to his home with all speed?" said the Jew questioningly.

"Nay, but I must find a hiding-place for him, and Bourne would be the first place where Sir Hubert's friends would expect to find him," said the knight; and then he looked keenly at the old Jew, fearing that he had said too much in his presence.

The old man seemed to understand the steadfast gaze, and for once he forgot his usual cringing manner, and said, in a tone of deep earnestness, "May the God of Abraham, Isaac, and Jacob do so to me, and the posterity of my people, if old Nathan betray the stranger who befriended him in his hour of need. Nay, nay, proud Norman, thou dost abuse the Jew while thou art robbing him; but truth and honor and gratitude have not wholly departed from Israel. If thy son is in danger give him to the care of old Nathan, and my life shall go for his life."

Lady de Valery uttered a faint scream at the bare proposal. "What! give my son to a dog of a Jew when his life may be in peril from this wound!" she exclaimed.

Her husband, however, gently led her to one side

THE POSTERITY OF MY PEOPLE: *my descendants*
BARE: *blunt*

of the pavilion, and whispered a few words in her ear. "We *must* accept this old man's proposal," he said, as he concluded. "The danger Guy is in from Sir Hubert's kinsmen is greater far than that of his wound, and for the sake of our other children we must seek some hiding-place for him far, far away from Bourne.

"The saints are fighting against us in all things," wailed the lady, wringing her hands with grief. Then turning to Adelais, who sat near, she asked if the embroidered cape promised to the prior of Crowland had been sent before they set out on their journey. Now Adelais had been too much occupied in looking after her own dress for this grand occasion to give much heed to any other finery, and so she could not give a very satisfactory reply. This seemed to increase her mother's grief and terror tenfold.

"The saints have been insulted, and their service neglected, and in anger they have withdrawn their protection from us. O, my son, my son! what evil hast thou done that a Jew should be chosen to protect thee instead of the blessed St. Dunstan and St. Thomas!" and the Lady de Valery gave herself up to the indulgence of her grief, while her husband and the old Jew went to make the needful preparations for Guy's removal in a litter.

Adelais tried to comfort her mother by proposing another pilgrimage to Canterbury, in which she herself would take part; but the lady refused to be comforted.

"It is of little use," she said; "I went barefoot, like the poorest pilgrim, and spent the night in tears and fasting by the blessed tomb, and thought that most surely St. Thomas à Becket would help and protect my son, and—"

"But, my mother, thou didst tell us that it was through the saint's mighty protection that Guy returned from the holy war in safety," interrupted Adelais.

"Yes, it was doubtless through his aid that he came back in safety," admitted the lady; "but did I not ask that he might be crowned with honor —might be the bravest knight in Europe next to King Richard? He hath won neither name nor fame; only dishonor hath fallen to his share; and, now that he is given into the hands of this Jew, evil and witchcraft will be his portion, for God and the blessed saints will wholly forsake him."

"Could none but a Jew protect him? Surely my father is bewitched to suffer this accursed old man, whose touch is pollution, even to approach him," exclaimed Adelais.

"They are an accursed race, but they above all men are skilled in the curing of wounds and the knowledge of balsams and medicaments, and, therefore, are they often sought for. They will by no means suffer this secret knowledge to be imparted to our monks and leech-men.

LEECH-MEN: *doctors*

"I would rather die than that a Jew should touch me," said Adelais scornfully; but it seemed that her father, at least, had well-nigh forgotten his prejudice against the Jews, for he presently returned, conversing familiarly with old Nathan, who seemed suddenly to have grown taller, and lost half the wrinkles from his yellow, parchment-skinned face.

"Now, thou knowest our bargain," said Sir Valence, as they drew near the spot where Guy was still lying unconscious. "I will pay thee two hundred zechins now, and when thou shalt bring me tidings that my son is safe beyond the sea I will pay thee two hundred more."

Lady de Valery would again have interposed if she could, and handed Guy over to the keeping of someone less objectionable than a Jew; but for once her husband was firm in having his own plans carried out. Most bitterly did the lady regret having engaged old Nathan to come with them. But, as usual, she blamed the saints for what had happened rather than herself. She said she supposed that some sin had been committed in her household, or the appointed fasts of the Church had not been duly kept, and therefore the saints had withdrawn their favor from her family. If the thought of God Himself ever came into the lady's mind, it was with a sort of shudder of apprehension and terror. He had been put so far out of sight, and the Church had interposed so many

mediators between the sorrowing, sinful soul of
man and the tender, pitiful Savior, who had died
to redeem men from their sin and sorrow, that it
was not strange Lady de Valery should turn from
the thought of God as from a hideous nightmare.
He was the stern, unrelenting Judge who would by
no means clear the guilty. True, there was the image of the blessed mother of mercy, with the child
Jesus in her arms, before which she sometimes
prostrated herself, in the minster church of Crowland. But the worship of Mary had never taken so
great a hold upon the mind of the northern na-
tions as it had in the south. The stern virtue of St.
Dunstan, or the bold fearlessness of St. Thomas
à Becket, had a far greater charm for the English
nation; and, therefore, it was not strange that their
ideas of God were fashioned after the pattern of
their favorite saints.

Lady de Valery kissed the pale face of Guy, and
then, sad-hearted, turned to prepare for her own
journey homeward, determined to look after her
household more closely, as well as to perform
her own religious duties more thoroughly. Poor,
heart-broken mother! how it must have grieved the
loving heart of the gentle Savior to see her thus
turning away from the only comfort that could
assuage such grief as hers! How greatly His love
was misunderstood! All that He had done and suffered was utterly ignored by those who professed
to know Him; and we wonder, as we read these

MEDIATORS: *go-betweens*
PITIFUL: *compassionate*
ASSUAGE: *relieve*

dark pages of history, how God, with all His long-suffering and patience, could bear to see those whom His own well-beloved Son had died to redeem thus groping in darkness, and turning farther and farther from Him, while they sought consolation and strength from the many earthly mediators and saviors set forth by their blind guides. But, looking back from our vantage ground in the nineteenth century, we can see, through the darkness of that time, "the form of One like unto the Son of God"[1] leading His people, although they knew it not. And as the philosophers of the day sought, by many a strange process, to turn the baser metals into gold, so God, the infinite Alchemist, used even the blunders and mistakes of our ancestors for their good; and in due time their race was transformed by the working of His mighty power into its present dignity and grandeur. We talk of the stern virtue and unyielding honesty of our Puritan forefathers, as though these noble traits came into the world with them, forgetting that they were the slow growth of ages—ages, too, of miserable blundering and misunderstanding, in which the world seemed to be almost entirely given up to the wicked one.

But poor Lady de Valery could descry nothing but vengeful anger in what had befallen her family. The curse of the Ericsons was the primal cause of all the trouble, she thought, and the saints had received some fresh cause of displeasure, and saints of such stern virtue as St. Dunstan, were not likely

---

[1] DANIEL 3:25

DESCRY: *see*
PRIMAL: *original*

to pass over a transgression without punishing it. She would hardly have believed, even though an angel from heaven had whispered it, that what she called a curse was the richest blessing God could bestow, and perhaps given, too, in answer to the prayers of the old monk whom his brethren deemed almost unworthy of Christian burial. In the later years of his life, when strictly shut up from all intercourse with the outer world, and from all but a few of the older brethren, Leofwine had devoted himself almost entirely to praying for his family and their children. Like Abraham, his cry had been, "O that they may live before thee!"[1] and God had heard and answered his prayer; for, while each had deplored his connection with the recreant monk, and his inheritance of the curse of the Ericsons, each had learned to know more fully than those by whom they were surrounded, the truth so dimly and darkly taught, that God loved the world—loved it even to the giving up His Son to die for its redemption.

The Saxon Bible, copied by this same old monk, had been in the family ever since it was first sent from Crowland minster, and as it had been read by each in turn it had been a great instrument in the Divine hand of teaching the Ericsons to look beyond the priest of Rome, even to the great High Priest Himself, for the pardon of sin. In various ways—by paths that they knew not—God had led them about, never giving any great earthly

[1] GENESIS 17:18

INTERCOURSE: *communication*

prosperity to this Saxon family, but imparting to each this "pearl of great price"[1]—the knowledge of His love.

But to each in turn this knowledge had come in apparently the most natural way. There had been no miracle wrought, no angel visitant sent to whisper the blessed secret that, "God so loved the world, that he gave his only begotten Son, that whosoever believeth in him should not perish, but have everlasting life."[2] Only these simple Saxon franklins had learned, one after another, to feel that the absolution for sin given by man did not meet their soul's need. The burden of sin had made itself felt as too irksome for the lightly uttered words to give peace and rest, and so, from priest and Church, they had turned to the old Saxon Bible, which they treasured as a family heirloom, although it was the gift of that monk who had brought the curse upon their race.

That a blessing and not a curse had been handed down to them from the humble brother, Leofwine, was more than half-suspected by several who, like Elfreda's father, chose for their battle cry, "Christ and His salvation;" but none had been bold enough to say this. With the Normans ruling in the land they were only too thankful to be left in peace to till their farm, and teach their children in secret the almost forgotten art of reading, that they, too, might profit by the treasure bequeathed to them; and so they were regarded by

[1] MATTHEW 13:46   [2] JOHN 3:16

IRKSOME: *troublesome*

their neighbors with a mingled feeling of pity, contempt, and fear, because the ban of the Church had been pronounced against them; and no one had yet been found pious enough, or powerful enough, to induce the Holy Father at Rome to remove the curse of the Ericsons.

So Lady de Valery returned to her castle-home groaning under its terrors, and vainly wishing Elfreda had never reached the shores of England; while Elfreda, viewing herself in a somewhat similar light, as the cause of all her friends' troubles, which she feared would never cease while she lived, had almost determined to commit self-destruction, hoping by this means to save Longbeard, at least, from the evil which now seemed his impending fate—an ignominious death as the leader of London's revolt.

Elfreda was prevented from putting this into execution only by her own sudden arrest and imprisonment—not, however, in the Tower, as she supposed. It soon transpired that she and Longbeard's wife had been seized by a party of friends, who saw this to be the only means of rescuing them from the power of the archbishop. This prelate had at last seized Longbeard, and condemned him to death, although his wife and family knew nothing of this at present; they had not even heard that he had been brought to trial, and fondly hoped still that King Richard would remember his promise, and interpose on his behalf. To Elfreda

SELF-DESTRUCTION: *suicide*
TRANSPIRED: *happened*

came the hardest portion of this trial, for it was decided that the friends must separate to avoid suspicion, and the family of old Nathan, the Jew, undertook the dangerous charge of concealing Elfreda. And so to the care of these despised people both cousins were entrusted, neither knowing of the other's danger until brought face to face in their friendly jailer's house.

Chapter XI

Another Crusade

WHEN Guy recovered from insensibility and the stupor that followed, he found himself in a place so utterly unlike anything that he had ever seen in England, that at first he thought he must be with King Richard again besieging the stronghold of Acre. His eye rested on the Oriental surroundings of the room. Halfway up the wall silken curtains and embroidered tapestry concealed the rough timbers and stone, while on the table stood a branched candlestick of solid silver, bearing several tiny lamps, which burned with a pale, steady flame, lighting up every corner of the little room. There were no chairs or benches, but a pile of cushions lay on the opposite side, which, with the table and candlestick, and one massive chest beside the couch, comprised the whole furniture of the place.

Guy was alone when he awoke, and had time to look round and notice each article of furniture. He then began to look for some signs of a window,

INSENSIBILITY: *unconsciousness*

for as his senses gradually returned he became conscious of a dull, roaring sound such as he remembered to have heard once before in his life, when the Jews incautiously ventured to enter Westminster Abbey. He tried to rise, but the attempt was a failure, as well as all his efforts to descry something like a window. He was trying to solve the puzzle of this strange apartment, so prison-like, yet so luxurious, when the arras at the foot of his couch was slowly pushed aside, and through a low arched door Elfreda entered the room.

"Where am I? Art thou a prisoner, Elfreda?" gasped Guy, again trying to raise himself.

"Hush, hush! thou art with friends, my cousin," said Elfreda.

Guy winced at the word "cousin," and tossed himself back on the couch. "Where am I?" he again demanded, looking steadfastly at Elfreda.

"Nay, but thou must be calm, or thy wound will bleed afresh. Thou art with friends—this is no prison, as thou mayest see," added Elfreda.

"But there is no window; and the noise I can hear—listen, Elfreda—what is that?"

Instead of listening, the poor girl put her fingers in her ears, and turned her head away to hide her tears and conceal her emotion.

But Guy would not be put off. "Thou must and shalt tell me what hath happened," he said excitedly, and, almost beside herself with grief and dismay, Elfreda fell on her knees beside the couch.

"It is the curse," she gasped; "the curse of the Ericsons that nothing can remove."

Guy looked at her, and then listened to the ominous sounds, while Elfreda knelt sobbing, until, with a sudden burst of anguish, she buried her face among the rushes on the floor, and exclaimed, "O, Guy, Guy, I have killed thee, too! old Nathan said thou were not to hear aught of this day's doings, or it would bring back thy sickness."

"Nay, nay, Elfreda, thou hast not killed me. I heard the noise of this London mob. We are in London, I trow," he added.

Elfreda nodded. "We are in the house of old Nathan, the Jew, who brought thee from Grantham."

In a moment Guy remembered all that had happened at the tournament—the falling of Sir Hubert and the cry of his friends. "Where are my mother and father?" he asked.

"They are safe," answered Elfreda, and she began to tell him all she knew concerning his being given into the care of old Nathan, who was considered a skillful physician, hoping by this means to divert his attention from the loud noises that penetrated even to this underground apartment.

Guy listened to her recital, but presently said, "There is a riot, Elfreda, or another murderous attack upon the Jews;" and then he suddenly asked, "Where is thy kinsman, Longbeard? I heard he was in some danger."

But at that question Elfreda's tears burst out

afresh, and she exclaimed passionately, "I would that I had died in Jerusalem, or could sacrifice my life now, to take this bitter curse away."

"Then Longbeard hath been brought to trial!" exclaimed Guy.

"Nay, I know not rightly what hath happened— only the streets are full of people and soldiers, and the church of St. Mary-le-Bow, where Longbeard hath sought sanctuary, hath been set on fire by order of the archbishop. I would that I had died before I had brought this evil upon him," sobbed Elfreda.

Guy would fain have comforted her, but what could he say—only that he would try to take this curse away so soon as he should recover from his wound.

That a serious relapse should follow upon the excitement of this first waking from a long unconsciousness was only to be expected, and it was many weeks before Guy heard the full particulars of that cruel day's work. How the Saxons, who had taken refuge in the church were forced by the smoke and flames to surrender themselves to the Norman soldiers, and how that William Longbeard, already severely wounded, was tied to the tail of a horse, and dragged to the Tower, and there, without even the formality of a trial, instantly executed. Little wonder was it that Elfreda lost her health and spirits, believing, as she did, that the secret cause of all this misery lay in her return from Jerusalem. Now, indeed, she was most anxious to leave England and all her friends, lest her staying here should bring more trouble upon them.

Old Nathan told Guy this, as he sat upon the pile of cushions, still looking pale and thin, but trying to put on some pieces of armor. The old man shook his head as he saw that his patient was as yet too weak to bear their weight.

"I feared it was too soon for thee to essay coat of mail yet," he said. "Thou art safe here, and though I say not but the cost of hiding thee hath been considerable, still, old Nathan is not ungrateful for the kindness shown to him, though he is but a poor old man—very poor, very poor."

"My father will repay thee every zechin I have cost thee," said Guy; "but now let us talk about our journey. Thou sayest Elfreda is eager to depart from London, and will journey with us to France. Whither wilt she go then?"

The old man shook his head. "I can send her to some of my people who will protect her for—for a consideration, for they, too, are poor; the Jews are a despoiled people now."

"Yes, yes, we know that," said Guy impatiently; "but thou sayest Elfreda will never see me again, and truly she hath kept her word for nearly a month; but thou knowest, good Nathan, that no damsel can travel alone, and Elfreda hath little store of zechins to reward thy extortionate people for their care of her."

ESSAY: *try, attempt*
EXTORTIONATE: *greedy*

"Elfreda hath that which thy mother bestowed upon her when she came to London. He who died for the cause of the poor and the defense of truth and freedom would not rob the orphan of a silver penny, and so it is that Elfreda hath store of zechins this day."

Guy looked both pleased and disappointed. To have provided for his cousin's wants, even though he never saw her face again, would have been the greatest joy to him; still, to hear that she had "store of zechins," to defend her from the cruel stings of poverty, was an intense relief, and, knowing her anxiety to leave London as soon as possible, he urged the Jew to commence the necessary preparations at once, saying he should be well enough to set out whenever they were ready.

During his convalescence Guy had ample time to think over his past life, and form some plan of action for the future; but beyond the resolution to go to King Richard's camp, and wield his sword in his service, he could think of no plan for the future. With the past, however, his thoughts were busy enough. Again and again did he recall the words of his confessor on the day of the tournament, when he felt so restless and excited; and when, instead of calmly recalling all his past sins, he could think only of some trifling circumstances that were better forgotten at such a time. The prior, too, had then told him that the Church could not absolve from unconfessed sins. Then

ABSOLVE FROM: *grant pardon for*

he thought of Sir Hubert, and of his sudden and mysterious death; and wondered whether or not he had been shriven before he entered the lists, and if not, was he guilty of sending this man before the great Judge with unconfessed sins upon his head.

The thought of this grew at last to be an intense misery to poor Guy, and he forgot everything that had led to the quarrel and challenge—everything but that Sir Hubert had been sent out of the world as little prepared in all probability as he himself would have been had he fallen. This thought had never troubled him before, although Sir Hubert was not the first his lance had hurried into eternity. In the quiet, solitary hours he spent in this underground chamber he had ample time to think of such subjects in all their bearings.

How glad he was to set off on his journey at last! He longed for action, to forget all the causes for anxiety that now burdened him; and what cared he if his life, like that of so many others, fell a sacrifice to this quarrel between Richard and Philip of France? Since Elfreda had forsaken him life was of little value; and so it was with a spirit of reckless despair that he at last reached King Richard's camp, and engaged anew in his service.

Meanwhile Elfreda had eluded the watchful eyes of both her cousin and the old Jew. She had long ago decided that only with the sacrifice of her life could the dreadful curse be taken away: and since the death of Longbeard this had seemed to her a positive duty; she only waited for a fitting opportunity to carry it into effect. There rose before her mind sometimes the dim recollection of hearing of a great Sacrifice for sin that had been made once for all—for the sins of the whole world—but surely her memory or her mind must be misleading her, for had she not heard again and again that this curse had never been removed from her family? and had she not seen proof of this in the calamities that had befallen Longbeard and the de Valerys?

So, using what precaution she could, Elfreda stole away from the party of travelers as soon as they landed on the coast of France, and, returning to the spot where they had left the boat, watched for an opportunity to jump into the water. Drowning seemed to be the only way open to her, so she crept down to the edge of the strand, and watched the waves as they beat against the sides of the boats, and wondered how long it would take to drown, and whether the dreaded curse would follow her beyond the waves, and hold her fast in that purgatory of which she had heard her confessor speak. Elfreda waited a long time, walking up and down, watching the restless waves and looking for an opportunity to dash herself in, unobserved by the fishermen and loiterers, who were standing about the beach. At length, however, the looked-for opportunity came, and she

STRAND: *beach*
BODKIN: *hairpin*

threw herself in, and was soon struggling with the waves.

In an instant she was rather roughly dragged out of the water, and carried by two men to a cottage close by. It was evident they supposed she had fallen in by accident; and the woman to whose care she was given bade her thank the saints and holy mother for her rescue. Seeing that she possessed one or two articles of value—a silver bodkin in her hair, and a silken kerchief round her neck, the good woman suggested that these should be presented to the sisters of the neighboring convent, and Elfreda, too weary and heartsick to resist her importunity, consented to their being carried thither at once, and also that the sisters should be informed of what had happened. The silver bodkin and kerchief brought two of the sisters to the cottage, and seeing how pale and worn poor Elfreda looked, they had her removed to the convent infirmary—for they were the only hospitals of those days—hoping that when her friends came to claim her they would bestow a liberal donation upon their rather poor house. But no one ever came to the convent gate to make inquiries, although Guy and old Nathan were busy looking for her in the town close by; so, when she got better, and had to face life once more, instead of death, as she hoped, she assumed the habit of a lay sister, thinking herself too unholy ever to become a professed nun. And so, while Guy helped King

IMPORTUNITY: *persistent demand*
HABIT: *robe*
LAY: *common*

Richard to carry on a desultory warfare against France, Elfreda tried to forget her sorrow in the humble duties of a lay sister—nursing the sick and caring for little children, carrying food to the poor in the time of distress, and comforting the widow and fatherless when some storm at sea robbed them of their earthly stay and protector.

Thus the years glided on, and King Richard died, and his brother John succeeded him as king of England; but there was little rejoicing except among his boon companions, and Guy preferred to live a wandering life in France rather than serve such a detested monarch as John. After awhile he took up arms in favor of William, Richard's nephew, and the rightful heir to the crown. This war was waged in France, and ended in 1200, when Guy joined Simon de Montfort, and with him went to hear the wonderful preaching friar at Neuilly, near Paris. Preaching was not common in those days, and so the excited harangues of Toulques, this new preaching friar, drew crowds of hearers. The theme he discussed was suited well to the times. It was neither more nor less than that another Crusade should be immediately undertaken. He had the people's warrant for urging men once more to take the sword from the scabbard, and many needed but little urging to do this.

A fresh impetus was given to this agitation a few months later, when Thibaut, lord of Champagne, suddenly announced, in the midst of a splendid

DESULTORY: *haphazard*
STAY: *support*
BOON COMPANIONS: *supporters*

tournament, that he was about to lay aside the *play* of martial life for the *duties* of chivalry. What duty could be so holy, so chivalrous, as wresting the sacred tomb from the power of the Turks? And so Thibaut pledged himself and all his vast wealth to aid this fourth Crusade, of which De Montfort was chosen the leader.

To transport this fresh crusading host to Palestine the aid of Venice must be sought. No other nation could boast of such a fleet as this little maritime republic. But Venice was by no means disposed to lend her ships on easy terms, and contrived to drive a pretty secure bargain. The stipulation was made that the money promised

WARRANT: *authorization*
MARITIME: *seafaring*

should be paid into the Venetian treasury before De Montfort's troops embarked. When the time came, however, and the crusaders had assembled at Venice, an unforeseen difficulty arose. Count Thibaut had died, and his heirs refused to hand over his wealth, so that the whole sum promised to the Venetians was not forthcoming. The doge refused to let them depart in his ships without an equivalent, and, having a war on hand himself, he adroitly engaged them to join him in this while on their way to the Holy Land, as an equivalent for their unpaid debt.

So with the wary old duke they went to Zara. Here they were met by another suppliant for their aid. A young Greek prince had been driven from Constantinople, and his father thrown into prison, while a usurper mounted the throne; and to regain this for his father he now besought the aid of these Christian knights. To many of the crusaders, however, the heretic Greeks were little better than Jews; for had they not refused to bow to the images of the blessed saints and the holy Virgin? Neither would they accept the authority of the holy father at Rome, but chose an archbishop, whom they called the patriarch, without even allowing the pope any voice in the selection. But Prince Alexis, in his distress, was willing to make any concession; and when it was made known to Pope Innocent that he had promised to submit the Greek Church to his authority and receive the laws and ritual of Rome

DOGE: *duke*
ADROITLY: *skillfully*
SUPPLIANT FOR THEIR AID: *person begging aid*

The Doge Refusing to Let the Crusaders Depart

for the government of the Church of Constantinople, he eagerly accepted the offer, and bade the
crusaders turn their arms against Constantinople
before proceeding to Palestine. To subdue the
Greek Church and bring it under the subjection
of Rome had been the dream of Pope Gregory the
Great, and each of his successors; but none had
seen the dream realized, and the insubordination
of the various European Churches had given each
pope quite enough to do. But the opportunity now
offered of extending her power was too favorable
for Rome to neglect.

The doge of Venice was quite willing to join in
this expedition for the sake of the spoil that would
fall to his share, and so the prows of the Venetian
galleys were turned toward the Bosphorus, and
the whole crusading army went wild with joy at the
thought of the treasure that would fall into their
hands from this fabulously rich and splendid city.

INSUBORDINATION: *disobedience*
THE BOSPHORUS: *the strait connecting the Black Sea with
    the Sea of Marmara*

Chapter XII

Guy de Valery's Vow

NEVER did more varied hopes and expectations animate a single army than now fired the martial courage of this crusading host as they at last anchored their vessels near the very gates of Constantinople, and caught a view of that wonderful city, so far famed, and yet so little known to Europeans. As the morning sun gilded the graceful domes of its churches and palaces, its library and other public buildings, each of which was a gem of art and a wonder in itself, the hearts of many beat high; but their hopes widely differed. To men like De Montfort, who were deeply and blindly devoted to serving the Church and increasing her power at all costs, the thought of imposing the Roman ritual on the recreant priests of the Orient, and bringing this gorgeous capital under the power of the pope, was the grand motive for action. To others, and among them the wary old doge of Venice, the prospect of the spoil that would fall into their hands—the treasure they could carry away from

ANIMATE: *inspire*

this storehouse of opulence—nerved them abundantly for the fight.

At first it seemed that the city would fall into their hands without resistance, for the enervated Greeks fled at the sight of the invaders; but the famous Veranger guard were not so easily beaten, and a series of skirmishes ensued wherever these appeared.

Guy fought with the land force led by De Montfort himself. In the midst of a fierce encounter near the gates, he, with a handful of his men, was cut off from the main body of the army and driven to some distance, where a hand to hand fight ensued. Most of the crusaders were left dead upon the field. Guy, however, had only fainted, and when, after some hours, he slowly recovered consciousness, it was to find himself alone, wounded and helpless, while night slowly veiled the turrets of the distant city from his sight. To die here in this fashion was worse than dying on the field of battle; so, after many fruitless efforts, he at last contrived to struggle to his knees. With feeble, fainting cry he prayed that the aid of some saint might be given him in this hour of extremity. He vowed that if his life was spared it should henceforth be devoted to the service of the Church. He would enter one of the military orders of monks, and, recalling his early wish on this subject, he vowed that he would become a Knight Hospitaler if only he were rescued from his perilous position.

OPULENCE: *great wealth*
ENERVATED: *weak*
HOUR OF EXTREMITY: *time just before death*

Scarcely had the prayer been uttered when a dim, shadowy form was seen approaching, and to Guy's excited fancy it was easy to believe that it was that of a saint just descended from heaven in answer to his prayer. He bowed his head among his dead companions, and when at length he raised it again it was to see an old man standing beside him, carrying a flask of wine and a small loaf of bread.

"My son, I give thee this in the name of Christ, in whom we both believe, although thou art not of our Greek Church," said the aged stranger, and, pouring out a portion of the wine in a little cup, he put it to Guy's lips. Seeing he was able to drink so well he gave him half the loaf, and then turned to look at the white, still faces of the wounded knight's companions to see if some of them needed the same restoratives. But they were all far beyond the reach of earthly needs, and the old man passed on without another word, leaving Guy in a sort of stupid wonder as to whether his deliverer was a saint or only a mortal man—a miserable monk of this heretical Greek Church. Strengthened by the wine and the bread, Guy contrived to creep toward the edge of the field, where he hoped some other stragglers from the army might see and help him. In this hope he was not disappointed. De Montfort himself, with a party of knights and esquires, soon passed that way, and by his orders a litter was speedily procured, and Guy was carried to a place of safety, where his wounds were dressed. Here, to his great grief, he had to stay until the close of the siege of Constantinople.

From the quiet spot where he lay he could see the lurid flames of the distant city. Nearly a third of Constantinople was on fire. Not only were matchless works of art, in stone and bronze and color, crumbling or melting or burning to ashes, but the accumulated work of learned men for ages past was also being consumed, and not less than ten thousand costly manuscripts perished in this conflagration.

Guy heard of this, but it made little impression upon him, for he cared as little as his companions for the learning that was slowly transforming the

LURID FLAMES: *horribly glowing flames*
CONFLAGRATION: *large, destructive fire*

world. What if the library was burned and a few thousand Greeks left homeless and destitute, so long as the Church was triumphant, and her ritual and laws imposed upon these heterodox Christians. The tidings that the Roman service had at last been performed in the chief churches seemed to have crowned the expedition with success, and the conquerors conveniently ignored the fact that they themselves were the only worshipers, and that a howling mob of Greeks groaned over this desecration of their churches by the Romanists.

The pope was informed of the triumph of the soldiers of the cross, and may have indulged some sanguine dreams about this conquest; but they were soon dispelled. Scarcely had the Venetian galleys, laden with the spoil of Constantinople and the small remnant of the crusading army left the Bosphorus, before every vestige of the hated accessories of this Roman creed had been torn from the churches, and the dethroned patriarch of the Greek Church once more restored to his chair of office. To go to Palestine with such an insignificant force as now remained was out of the question, and so, to Guy's great disappointment, he heard that this Crusade was to be abandoned, at least for the present.

Having sufficiently recovered from his wounds to be able to follow his own will in regard to his future plans, Guy resolved upon taking the first steps toward the fulfillment of his vow, by retiring from

HETERODOX CHRISTIANS: *Christians with different beliefs*
VESTIGE: *trace*
CREED: *set of beliefs*

the world to the seclusion of a monastery before entering as an esquire the holy order of Knights Hospitalers. Hitherto he had used only earthly weapons against the enemies of the Church, but during his late sickness the question had been pressed more closely home, and he began to see that the evil in himself must be fought against and conquered before he could hope to accomplish the greater work of removing this curse from his family which brought so much misery upon them.

But to Guy religion seemed scarcely worthy the name unless it partook of the character of single combat with evil. The shield of faith and the sword of the Spirit must be almost as tangible as the weapons he had used in the service of King Richard. And so to begin this spiritual warfare what better course could he adopt than to seek admission among the most rigidly regulated brethren, that he might be helped by their example and discipline in his conflict with the world, the flesh, and the evil one. After spending a short time in Paris with his friend and leader, De Montfort, he retired to Fontaines, and entered the Cistercian monastery founded by an Englishman, who had introduced a much more strict rule of discipline than was usual in the other monasteries of France.

At Citeaux the monks had but one meal a day, and that only after having risen twelve hours from their beds, sung psalms, attended several services in the church, and worked in the fields. Here St.

PARTOOK: *took the form*

Bernard, who roused all Europe to undertake the Second Crusade, had spent the earlier years of his life, and many stories were told among the brethren of his wonderful piety and great faith. One of the old monks was never weary of telling the story of Bernard's departure with twelve of the brethren to found a new monastery in any spot God might choose:

"I was but a lad then," said he, "a novice; but our good abbot, Stephen Harding, granted me the great favor of being present in the church to witness the departure of our beloved brother Bernard. He was very young to be sent on such an errand, and feeble, too, from the austerities he had practiced—too frail and feeble to be sent forth into the wide world, not knowing where food or shelter were to be found; at least so thought many of the brethren as they gathered in the church with tearful eyes and sorrowful faces.

The good abbot, Stephen, blessed them after prayers, and then, placing a cross in brother Bernard's hands, he bade him go forth and plant a colony of Cistercian monks wheresoever they were needed. No directions were given or asked. Some of the brethren accompanied the travelers to the limit of our own lands, while others stayed in the church to pray for God's direction and blessing on the new community."

"And did Bernard succeed?" asked Guy.

The old monk looked up in surprise at the

AUSTERITIES: *harsh self-denial*

question. "Hast thou never heard of the Abbot of Clairvaux, who hath performed many wonderful miracles in his lifetime, besides disputing with the heretic Abelard, and preaching with such eloquence that the haughtiest kings and princes were ready to lay down their crowns, and the poorest weavers and soldiers their lives, to fight the Lord's battle in the Holy Land?"

The old man looked rather disdainfully at Guy, but pitying his ignorance he afterward volunteered to give him a history of the theological dispute between Bernard and Abelard, an offer Guy accepted, but did not derive much profit from. To mortify his body by fasting and long-continued labor—to struggle against the world and the evil one, which to him was the continued remembrance of his gentle cousin Elfreda—was what he longed to accomplish; but the struggle threatened to be a long one. Weary months passed, and found him still far from having attained that peace he thought must follow upon his victory: a victory over self that must be gained before he could even enter as an esquire into the holy order of Hospitalers. To Guy this was included in his vow, and bitter was his disappointment when the superior of the monastery one day bade him relax some of his self-imposed austerities, which were now seriously threatening to undermine his health.

"Thou hast come to this holy house to profit by

SUPERIOR: *head*

the examples of the brethren; thou must learn, therefore, to obey even as they do; but I would say more, though not as a command, but as wholesome advice. Thou art not coming to spend thy life within these walls, but to do God's service in the world; thou, therefore, hast the more need of thy strength, and it were better for thee to depart ere long to do the work of a chivalrous knight than to abide here longer than is needful for the subduing of the flesh."

Guy went from the presence of the superior deeply humbled. How great a sinner he must be, for although he had spent all these months in almost ceaseless devotion, and the practice of the greatest severities he could inflict upon his body, he was no nearer gaining what he sought; and yet the superior evidently thought the time he had been there was long enough for this purpose. Sometimes, in his dreams, it seemed to him that the Virgin mother drew near to assure him of her forgiveness; but before the vision faded, the face had assumed the well-known lineaments of his cousin Elfreda, and then there would come back to his mind those first words she had spoken to him, "Christ and His salvation."

After such a dream as this Guy was sure to redouble his austerities, for was it not a temptation of Satan to be fought against—this remembrance of his cousin—and yet, try as he would, he could not banish her from his thoughts. If he only knew

LINEAMENTS: *features*

where she was—what had become of her after she left old Nathan—he thought he could succeed better in conquering this persistent memory of her; but as it was, his mind was more occupied with this now than ever it had been before. This, and the death of Sir Hubert de Grantham, weighed more heavily on his conscience than anything else, although his consciousness of other sins was by no means feeble. But neither for the real nor for the imaginary sins of which he had, or thought he had, been guilty, could Guy find any remedy—"To give his guilty conscience peace."

Fastings and penances, following the strictest rules of the monks, seemed powerless to lift this heavy load of sin from his heart; and yet he was accounted almost a saint by the brethren. At last he thought that it might be the terrible hereditary curse which prevented his gaining the desired peace, and this fancy drove him from his retirement, and he resolved to enter the order of Hospitalers without further delay. Might it not be that in the fulfillment of his vow to the very letter he should find the peace he sought in vain elsewhere?

There was little difficulty in persuading the Grand Master of one of the preceptories near Paris to grant admission to one of Guy's rank and renown—for as a crusader and a follower of the devoted De Montfort his character was established—and arrangements were soon made for his formal admission.

PRECEPTORIES: *communities of Knights Hospitaler*

On the day appointed, the knights of all the preceptories for some miles round assembled in the church, where the Grand Master, in full flowing robes of white, sat near the altar, ready to receive the aspirant. After prayers had been offered, and several psalms sung, Guy drew near the steps of the altar to repeat the prescribed vow:

"I do promise to Almighty God, to the holy eternal Virgin Mary, the mother of God, and St. John the Baptist, to render henceforward, by the grace of God, perfect obedience to the superior placed over me by the choice of the order, be he who he may; to live without personal property; and to preserve my chastity."

The Grand Master then rose. "We acknowledge thee as the servant of the poor and sick, and as having consecrated thyself to the defense of the Catholic Church," and as he spoke he delivered the missal into Guy's hands.

Bowing his head reverently, he kissed the book, saying these words, "I acknowledge myself as such," and then carried it to the altar, which he also kissed, kneeling. Then he brought the missal back and delivered it again to the Grand Master, who stood ready to invest him with the robes of the order.

Pointing to the white cross on the front of the mantle, he said, "Dost thou believe, my brother, that this is the symbol of that holy cross on which the Savior died for our redemption?"

ASPIRANT: *someone who desires to do something*
MISSAL: *book of prayers*
INVEST: *clothe*

"Yes, I do verily believe it," answered Guy.

"This is likewise the sign of our noble order," went on the Grand Master, "which we command thee to wear;" and as he spoke he threw the mantle around Guy's shoulder so that the cross rested on the left side of his breast.

Guy then kissed the sacred symbol, and received a kiss from the Grand Master, who said, "Receive this sign in the name of the Holy Trinity, of the holy Virgin Mary, and of St. John the Baptist, for the increase of the faith, the defense of the Christian cause, and the good of the poor. We place this cross on thy breast, my brother, that thou mayest love it with all thine heart; and may thy right arm ever fight in its defense, and for its preservation. Should it ever be that in combating against the enemies of the faith thou shouldst retreat, desert the standard of the cross, and take to flight, thou wilt be stripped of this truly holy sign, as having broken the vow thou hast just taken, and thou wilt be cut off from our body as a corrupt and unsound member."

Then, tying the robe around his neck, he said, "Receive the yoke of the Lord, it is easy and light, and thou wilt find rest for thy soul. We promise thee nothing but bread and water, a simple habit of little worth, but we give thee and thy parents and kindred a share in the good works performed by our order, and by our brethren, both now and hereafter, throughout the world."

To all this Guy devoutly responded, "Amen, so be it."

Surely he would now obtain "rest for his soul,"[1] and the curse would be lifted from his family at last; for the superabundant good works of this mighty order would be more than sufficient to secure this, and had he not just received the promise of a share in these "good works?" These were Guy's thoughts as he received the salutations of the brethren.

[1] Matthew 11:29

salutations: *greetings*

Chapter XIII

The Lay Sister

THE passing years brought little change to the humble lay sister, Elfreda. She heard of the death of King Richard, and the accession of John, and she often thought of her cousin, wondering whether he still lived. Living or dead, it would make little difference to her, she often whispered to herself; and now, far away from her friends, they, perhaps, might be happy, and she would bear the burden of this curse alone.

The excitement that followed the preaching of the Fourth Crusade reached, with its outermost ripple, this poor little convent on the coast, and the sisters gave what help they could—their prayers, and a few crowns realized by the sale of some needlework. To Elfreda, however, it brought additional work in nursing the sick, for a number of knights passed through the town who had recently landed from England, bringing with them the usual camp followers—cheapmen and Jews, mountebanks, gleemen, and beggars; and among

MOUNTEBANKS: *sellers of quack medicines who attracted customers by telling stories*
GLEEMEN: *minstrels*

this motley crowd sickness had broken out, and so the sisters of the convent soon had their hands full in preparing food and medicine for those who had thus been brought to their doors.

Among these was an old man, dressed in a tattered gabardine and soiled yellow cap, from whom everybody shrank. The poor fellow must have perished had not Elfreda heard one of her companions speaking of him, and his daring audacity in presuming to come among Christians.

"Is he a Jew, this old man?" asked Elfreda; and then she added, "I will go and see him. I am only a poor lay sister, and so I do not mind coming into contact with him."

The others looked at each other, and then at her. "Thou art very strange! More strict in thy fasts and penances than a professed nun, and taking all the disagreeable work of nursing upon thee from choice, and yet thou sayest thou hast no hope of ever being a holy saint."

"No, I can never be a saint," said Elfreda, shaking her head sadly, and thinking how very, very far off she was, and ever would be, from attaining that distinction while she carried the burden of this terrible family curse. "No, I can never hope to be a saint. I shall be content if, through having a share in the prayers and good works of the holy sisterhood, I escape purgatory; so I think I will visit this old Jew."

As she went out of the convent kitchen her companions turned to look after her, shaking their

AUDACITY: *bold disregard for restrictions*

heads and shrugging their shoulders.

"I wish she was not so dreadfully good," said one.

"Yes, she does so much that the superior thinks we ought to do the same. I wish something would happen to take her away from our convent, and I know somebody else who would be glad to escape Sister Elfreda's sharp eyes."

"Who is that?" asked two or three together.

But the sister shook her head. "Nay, nay," she said, "I may not tell thee that, but we will see if there is a chance of ridding ourselves of—"

But here she was suddenly interrupted by the entrance of a nun, who in a sharp voice commanded her to go on with her work.

Meanwhile Elfreda had reached the little hovel where the old Jew had been laid, and on bending over him saw, to her astonishment, that it was old Nathan. She started and trembled as she held a little wine to his lips; but the old man did not recognize her. Indeed, he was too ill for some days to notice anything that was passing around him, and when at last he woke up to the reality of life once more, he wanted to get up and recommence his journey. Although scarcely able to lift his head from the straw pillow, he was struggling to raise himself to a sitting posture when Elfreda entered.

"Nay, nay, thou art not strong enough to get up yet, good Nathan," said Elfreda, hastening forward.

The old man dropped upon his pillow at the sound of her voice and hearing his own name

RECOMMENCE: *begin again*

spoken. At length, after looking at her intently while she unpacked the little basket of food she had brought, he said with a slow emphasis, "Now the God of Abraham be praised, it is Elfreda, the Saxon orphan!" and then noticing her dress, he added, "Thou hast entered this convent, I trow."

"Nay, I am not good enough to be a nun. I am only a lay sister, whose work it is to succor such as thou," replied Elfreda.

The old man looked at her as she gently raised him to take the food she had brought. "Didst thou know I had a goodly store of zechins entrusted to me for thy use?"

But Elfreda cared little to hear of this. "I need not this money," she said; "but hast thou heard of Guy de Valery of late?"

"Not since he left me at the camp of King Richard. How camest thou here, Elfreda?"

"I have not left this place since thou and Guy brought me hither," answered Elfreda, a faint color stealing into her pale face as she recalled the day when she made an attempt to drown herself. She never could think of this now without bitter pain and self-reproach, for she had begun to see that it was a sin to try to escape from life instead of bearing its burdens.

"But could'st thou not leave this convent, since thou art only a lay sister?" asked old Nathan anxiously.

Elfreda shook her head. "Nay, I can never go back to England," she said.

Belial: *Satan*

"Nay, I would not counsel any to go to that land while this son of Belial, King John, doth rule there. I have left London forever, I trow, for the children of my people have found in the south of France a goodly land to dwell in—a land of vine and fig-trees, a land of plenty and liberty, even for the poor Jews. Ah, 'tis a goodly land, this Provençe and Languedoc," concluded old Nathan.

"And art thou going thither when thou art well?" asked Elfreda.

"Nay, but I must go there to get well. I am an old man, Elfreda, and I need warm sunshine. My people, too, have borne my few zechins and jewels with them, and I would fain join them as speedily as may be."

"But thou canst not take this journey alone, weak and ill as thou art," said Elfreda.

"No, not alone, and Nathan is a poor man; but if thou wouldst journey with me I have that in my pouch that will pay for all our wants. I could sit upon a horse, and with thee on the pillion behind, the old Jew would be safe both from enemies and sickness."

Elfreda looked at him in open-eyed wonder; but it was evident that Nathan was in earnest, whimsical as the idea seemed. Perhaps the old man had seen enough to convince him that Elfreda was not happy in her chosen life, and thought that this sunny land of Provençe, more like her childhood's home among the Jewish hills, would restore the pretty bloom to her rounded cheek, and make her

PILLION: *a seat for a lady placed behind the saddle*
WHIMSICAL: *strange*

more like the Elfreda he first saw when he went to ask counsel of William Longbeard.

Elfreda herself scarcely knew what to say to the old man's proposal. She owed him a debt of gratitude, not only on her own behalf, but for kindnesses he had shown to others of her family, and so, scarce daring to refuse his request outright, she promised to consult the superior of the convent upon the matter, telling her all the reasons she had for thinking it her duty to show every kindness to old Nathan, although he was a Jew.

Something like a satirical smile parted the nun's lips as she looked at Elfreda, but at last she said, "It were well for thee to depart from this house since thou wilt not become a professed sister of our order; but, nathless, we will not forsake thee or leave thee to the misbelieving Jews. I will give thee letters to bear to a holy house of sisters at St. Gilles, not far from Toulouse, and there thou mayest abide."

Elfreda hardly knew whether to be glad or sorry at this summary dismissal from what had been, perhaps, a monotonous round of hard work, that yet had brought many moments of comfort—almost happiness—when those whom she nursed blessed her for her kindness. They at least were sorry when they heard of Elfreda's departure, but old Nathan was exceedingly glad, and would have begun his journey at once if it had been possible.

At length they were able to set out toward the "sunny land of liberty," as old Nathan loved to call

SATIRICAL: *mocking*
SUMMARY: *quick*

it. "Even priests and monks live there who do not scorn poor Jews," said the old man, and he scarcely allowed himself the needful rest, so eager was he to press on and reach his destination.

The cause of this was not far to seek, for the old man's frequent mutterings of "jewels," "zechins," "embroidery," and "silver crowns," convinced Elfreda that from some cause he was anxious as to the safety of his wealth which friends had carried forward for him.

At length the soft, warm breeze began to tell them they were nearing the beautiful land of Provence—the land of poetry and luxury, where troubadour minstrels struck their harps and composed their lays, where life was one round of luxury and pleasure, and nothing higher than being crowned in the courts of love by the queen of beauty seemed to engage the attention of the most aspiring.

Elfreda was amazed, as she walked through the streets of Toulouse, to see Jews as richly dressed as any, and with scarcely any distinctive badge, walking among the other citizens, and elbowing their way through the crowd without any fear of touching them. In London they kept as much as possible to their own quarter of the town, and when compelled by business to come beyond its boundaries, they took care to seek the shelter of a wall, or crept along under the projecting eaves, anxious to escape notice, and careful not to contaminate their fellow-citizens by coming in contact with them. The contrast in this respect was very remarkable to Elfreda.

But this was not the only difference that she noticed between these people of the sunny south and the people in whose land she had birth. There seemed to be the same lightness and *insouciance* in their manner of worship as in all else; and although the ritual of the Church service was the same as that to which she had always been accustomed, the words of prayer seemed to trip off the lips of the priests, and the very chants to have a ring of troubadour minstrelsy about them. The troubadours, indeed, were never too devout, but loved to ridicule the Church and the clergy, high and low being alike treated with witty satire. And these merry and sarcastic glees were sung in the streets, nay, even openly joined in by the monks and priests themselves.

All this Elfreda saw during the few days she stayed with her friends, the Jews, and which they explained by saying that the Provençals never could be serious about anything. Life itself was only a holiday, to be enjoyed as much as possible while it lasted. Then they told witty stories of priests and monks forgetting altogether the duties of their sacred office, and joining in the contests at the courts of love, sometimes running to greater "excess of riot"[1] than the courtiers themselves. Elfreda looked shocked.

[1] I PETER 4:4
INSOUCIANCE: *carelessness*
TRIP: *dance*
GLEES: *songs*

"Surely the holy father should be informed of these evil doings," said she, "and the bishop be admonished to remove these priests."

"Nay, nay; the holy father will not trouble himself about those who merely seek to enjoy themselves. There are others in this place who are far more dangerous to the interests of holy Church."

"More dangerous than light-minded priests!" exclaimed Elfreda: "more wicked than this luxurious court of Count Raymond's!"

The Jewess who was telling her these stories of Provençal life shrugged her shoulders. "I said not that they were wicked; they are called the 'good men,' the 'perfect,' and some call them 'Vaudois,'[1] because they come from the valleys of the Alps."

"But if they are 'good men' surely they cannot be the enemies of holy Church!" exclaimed Elfreda.

The Jewess shook her head. "I know not what their belief may be, only that it is different from the teaching of holy Church, and many citizens have joined themselves to them because of their simple, blameless lives, though the priests say they are heretics, and must ever dwell in the pains of some dread fire after death, while a curse rests upon all who belong to them here."

Elfreda shuddered as she thought how the curse had fallen upon her family through the monk who had been called a heretic, and she resolved to

[1] The Vaudois, also known as Waldensians, were Christians who lived in the valleys of the Alps and later joined with Calvin and the reformers in Geneva.

avoid these "good people," for fear they should try to teach her their evil ways.

There was little to attract Elfreda in the luxuriously furnished house or the gay inmates. She could not forget that they were of an inferior race—"only Jews"—although they were wealthy, and joined in so many of the gay doings of the city.

And so, to old Nathan's great disappointment, Elfreda resolved to go to the convent of St. Gilles, assured that she should find there the peace and rest she could never hope for in this busy household. But before she went she bade old Nathan send for her if ever he were ill or needed her presence. "I shall only be a poor lay sister, thou knowest, and so it will be my duty to tend the sick, and they will let me come to thee."

"May the God of Israel bless thee for all the kindness thou hast shown me, Elfreda! I am an old man, a very old man, and the ways of my people here are strange to me. Though the sky is as bright and blue as that which shines above our sacred city, I sometimes wish I were in London, walking on the banks of the muddy little Fleet rather than sitting on this marble terrace, with its perfume of roses and orange trees, and—"

"Nay, nay; thou wilt soon learn to love this place; it is very beautiful," said Elfreda.

But the old man shook his head. "I shall miss thee, miss thee very sorely. And the zechins, Elfreda—thou knowest I have them still."

INMATES: *residents*

"Thou mayest keep them; I cannot touch them. Nay, nay; ask me not to take them."

"Thou art foolish, child, very foolish, for the zechins are good—money is very good," added the old Jew with twinkling eyes; but he did not press her to take the money again.

"Nathan will keep it a little longer," he said softly to himself. "He can make it a power in this city, and by and by—by and by—" The old man raised his eyes to heaven as he spoke, and slowly rose from his seat: "O God of Abraham and Isaac, thou wilt not always forsake us! thou wilt restore us to our own land, and the wealth we are now getting so slowly, so painfully, from the spoils of these Gentiles, shall be dedicated to thee—to the building of thy city and thy temple."

It was the first time Elfreda had ever heard this secret hope of the Jewish nation openly expressed. Nathan had sometimes hinted that his nation's intense love of gain was not the mere vulgar love of hoarding—that a secret, sacred hope inspired them—a hope they might long wait in vain to see accomplished, but which was yet sure and certain.

Now that she heard what this was she could only feel an intense pity for the old man, for at Jerusalem the Jews were more hated, more despitefully used, than even in England, and this by both Christians and Saracens; so that the world must become almost a new world before they could hope to have their claim recognized by these contending foes.

But she would not say a word to check the old

man's joy, for she could see, as the light breeze lifted his thin white hair, that a tear was glistening in his eye, and his face lost the look of deep cunning that was so habitual to it, and became almost glorified from the feeling of intense triumphant rapture that shone in it.

Elfreda saw that the old man had forgotten her and all external objects in the contemplation of his people's restoration, and she quietly crept from the room feeling more respect for the Jews as a people than she could have thought possible. As for old Nathan himself, her heart almost yearned toward him, for were they not akin in their sorrows? He was bearing the curse of his people, and she the curse of her family.

Chapter XIV

At the Convent

ELFREDA set out the next day for St. Gilles. Old Nathan insisted upon sending an escort with her. This was needful, for, as his friends informed him, a nun's dress was little protection from the aggressions of the gay multitude, if they happened to be bent on a frolic; and just now everybody was holding high festival, for the harvest promised to be very plentiful. The fields of maize and flax looked beautiful in the summer sunshine, while everywhere roses peeped out from the shelter of green leaves, or thrust themselves wantonly in people's faces as they passed the fragrant hedges or through the bowery lanes. Truly, it was a lovely land—this Languedoc—and little wonder was it that its people were so gay and light-hearted; only Elfreda sighed as she said this, and felt thankful that there were convents for sad-hearted people like herself.

Her Jewish escort left her as they came within sight of the convent of St. Gilles, and Elfreda

WANTONLY: *playfully*
BOWERY: *shaded*

hurried forward to the little postern and presented her letter of introduction. The lay sister who took it shook her head as Elfreda spoke a few words of explanation, and it was evident she could not understand what she said; but she opened the gate, and by sign invited her to take a seat on the stone bench inside, while she carried the letter in to the superior.

"This is France, and yet the people speak another language," whispered Elfreda softly to herself, for this was not the first time her French had not been understood.

But in a few minutes the sister returned, bringing a nun with her who, to Elfreda's great relief, spoke in the language of the North. "Thou hast come from Normandy, I trow?" she said in a pleasant voice.

Elfreda rose and bowed. "I am a lay sister, not a nun," she said quickly, fearing lest any mistake should be made about this matter.

"Thy letter will doubtless explain this," returned the nun. "Our superior, with most of the sisterhood, is out at this time; but I will bid thee welcome in her name; and, as thou art doubtless hungry, thou mayest follow me to the refectory, where we are even now at our evening meal."

Elfreda had learned the humble duty of a lay sister too well to venture to reply more than by an inclination of the head, and, following the nun, she was soon ushered into a pleasant, well-lighted hall, where some half-dozen nuns and one or two

REFECTORY: *dining hall*

lay sisters sat at their evening meal, while one
read aloud from a book. The tables were pretti-
ly adorned with vases of flowers, and there were
plates of fruit, and savory smelling meats, and tankards of wine.

Elfreda shut her eyes for a moment, and then
looked again, feeling sure her senses must have
deceived her, or that she had by some mistake got
into the hall of a castle instead of the refectory
of a convent—for anything more utterly unlike
what she had been accustomed to could not well
be imagined. But she soon found herself seated
at one of the long tables, and a loaded platter of
the savory food before her, while at the same time
she was invited to help herself to wine from the
tankard placed near.

After eating a little, Elfreda ventured to look
round upon her companions, for the reading had
recommenced, and everybody seemed more intent
upon listening to the reader's voice than eating or
noticing her. She saw, too, that they were drinking water, although they invited her to take wine.
Then she looked round the room, so different
from the bare, dim, cold refectory she had been
accustomed to, and began wondering where the
superior and the rest of the sisterhood could be,
and wishing the bell would ring for *vespers*.

But the reading continued for some time longer,
and the remnants of the meal were not cleared
away until the shadows began to deepen, and then
all, without any distinction, set to work at once to

VESPERS: *evening prayers*

remove the platters and tankards; and this was scarcely over before the door opened, and another party of nuns appeared.

"Now, you dull, perfect people, what have ye been doing while we have been out," asked one, speaking in Norman French.

"Hush! hush!" whispered a nun, pointing to Elfreda, and the fresh comers all stared at her with looks of silent curiosity for a minute or two. But her presence was soon forgotten again, for everyone seemed bent on hearing herself talk; and there was soon such a babel of tongues as only a party of women can create—such a merry clatter as Elfreda had never heard in the Northern convent during her whole residence there.

She could not understand all that was said, but she comprehended enough to know that most of these serge-clad nuns had been to a village festival, and some of them had even engaged in dancing, and were boasting of it, too. This boasting was speedily checked by the more grave sisters—those who had remained at home; while others laughingly reminded their companions that penance day was coming. But one of them had pushed her hood aside, and, with flushed and heated face, declared she would talk about the festival as long as she pleased.

"I care not for penance. Why should I do anything so disagreeable when the sweet mother of mercy is ready to forgive all we like to confess,"

BABEL OF TONGUES: *confusion of voices*

she said, with an occasional hiccup that provoked a laugh from her companions.

"Sister Annunziata hath been drinking of last year's grapes," whispered one.

"It is only her cup of comfort," remarked another, but no one seemed shocked, or even surprised; only one of those who had remained at home persuaded her to let her lead her to her cell, and then by degrees the others went off in the same direction, until at last Elfreda was left with those who had first welcomed her.

"Wilt thou go to rest now?" asked the one who had first spoken to her; "our lady superior cannot see thee tonight."

"Will there be no *vespers*—no prayers in the chapel?" asked Elfreda, in her amazement. A faint color stole into the nun's face: "Our house is somewhat disordered through this festival, and therefore there can be no service in our chapel; but we who are here will commit ourselves to God's care, and if thou dost desire it thou mayest stay."

"Thank you, I shall sorely miss the *vespers*; but if I may tarry awhile, I would fain join with you in prayer to God."

The nun bowed, and then spoke a few words to her companions, and one of them fetched a book, and presently began to read in the Latin tongue—the language of the Church in all countries. Elfreda sat and listened, but was thinking more of the strange scene she had witnessed a few minutes before than of what was being read, until something in the reader's manner caused her to give her undivided attention to this legend of the saints, as she supposed the account to be. But by degrees it broke upon her mind that this story was strangely familiar, although she could not remember when or where she had heard it before; but, like some half-forgotten strain of sweet melody, it awoke an answering echo in her mind, and her heart was thrilled with the sweet words of divine comfort. Wholly forgetful of where she was, she started as the reader paused, and then, in a voice half-choked by tears and emotion, she said:

"May it please thee to read that once more? I have heard it before, but I would fain hear it again lest I should forget it."

With a look of pleased surprise the reader began again, and Elfreda, as she listened and drank in the meaning of the words, suddenly remembered the old Saxon Bible at her uncle Ericson's, and how she had read there words like these: "Let not your heart be troubled." She remembered it all now. In a moment the scene rose before her mental vision—the proud Lady de Valery coming in at that moment, so that the book had to be closed, and until now she had never known what the next words were. She had read through the previous chapter, as the present reader had done, but nothing had seemed to rivet her attention like these words, "Let not your heart be troubled;"

and now her mind did not seem able to get beyond the next clause, "Ye believe in God, believe also in me."[1] What they might mean she did not know. She had discovered from the previous reading that it was the Lord Christ who was speaking, and she listened intently, thinking that some mention of the Virgin mother would follow, but there was none; and afterward, when the nuns kneeled down to pray, she could not but remark again that her name was omitted, as well as that of the saints usually invoked.

It was a strangely simple prayer, not at all like those used by the Church, for these nuns asked for grace and strength to be faithful. This seemed to be the whole burden of it, so far as Elfreda could understand, and it puzzled her as much as anything that she had yet seen; for surely these few abiding at home and quietly reading such books as they did were more faithful to their monastic vows than the light-minded sisters who had, in defiance of all rule and Church authority, been delighting themselves with the pleasures of the world. And yet these were praying for the pardon of sin and to be kept faithful, while the others seemed to have no fear upon the matter.

It was certainly a strange, confused, puzzling little world—this convent of St. Gilles—and the more Elfreda saw of it the less able she seemed to understand it. She was summoned to the superior's room the next day, and the sister who had

[1] JOHN 14:1

REMARK: *notice*

admitted her was questioned in a sharp, angry voice as to what she knew of her coming, and why she had suffered her to enter those sacred walls. The nun answered meekly and truly enough, giving her every detail she had heard from Elfreda, and pointing to the letter of introduction as she spoke; but it was clear that for some unknown cause she had fallen under the lady superior's displeasure, for she was instantly commanded to leave the room, and a severe penance was imposed upon her.

Elfreda thought she should be instantly dismissed for daring to intrude upon their holy house, but, to her surprise, she was told she could remain, and was dismissed to the garden, that being apparently the easiest mode of disposing of her. No duties were assigned her, and she went down to wander among the brilliant parterres of flowers—for the garden here was no mere growing-place for herbs and vegetables, but a luxurious pleasure-ground, with arbors and summer-houses, and luxurious seats placed in every cool, shady nook.

Seating herself in one of these, where she could watch the groups of nuns wandering up and down the green alleys, or sitting in the arbors, she gave herself up to thinking over the reading she had heard the previous night, wisely trying to forget for the present the puzzling questions that had arisen in her mind concerning the lax rule of this

PARTERRES: *gardens*

convent, and the easy, luxurious lives these nuns seemed to live.

Again she repeated the words, "Ye believe in God, believe also in me;" and then she asked herself the question, "Do I not believe in the Lord Christ? I know He is the Son of God—the Son of the blessed Mary, ever virgin; that she pleads with Him on behalf of poor sinners who dare not approach His holy presence by themselves. I believe all this. Can—"

But here her reverie was suddenly interrupted by the sound of voices close at hand. It seemed that two nuns had seated themselves on the other side of the myrtle copse, and, though neither could see the other, Elfreda could hear distinctly every word that was said, for they spoke in Norman French for greater security against listeners.

"Thou sayest that we are suspected of learning this strange doctrine taught by the Vaudois or 'good men,'" said one of the nuns rather anxiously.

"I greatly fear it is so, and that our superior will punish Sister Ave for teaching us. That is why she is condemned to so severe a penance this morning, I am sure."

"And yet our rule is so lax that I have heard it whispered that the bishop will be informed if the scandals concerning this house do not cease. Why should our—"

"Nay, but the bishop would be more displeased

if he heard that this doctrine of the Vaudois had found entrance here," replied her companion hastily.

"But what were we to do? I came here because—because the world seemed to have nothing in it worth living for after my Jacques died. I thought that in the Church I should surely find rest and peace, but I found that pleasure of some sort or other, varied with a little scandalous gossip and a good deal of envy and evil-speaking, was all I could hope to find here—at least, until Sister Ave and thou taught me that these nuns, and even the Church itself, had made a great mistake, and that we must go to God Himself; that the Lord Jesus Christ was waiting to bless and help such poor, tired, disappointed souls as mine, and needed no persuading by His mother or the saints to undertake it for us, since He had, out of pure love, died to redeem us from our sins."

"Hush, hush!" said her more prudent companion, for the speaker had raised her voice in utter disregard of the dangerous topic she was discussing.

"Nay, but I cannot hush! I wish every sister in this house would come and listen to me. I feel as though I were guilty of deceiving them when I hear them talking as Sister Annunziata did this morning about penances and the pity of the Virgin."

"Why, what did she say?" asked the other, anxious to divert her attention from the more dangerous subject.

"Someone had been telling her that she had drunk too much wine last night, and committed many sins while half-insensible."

"A story she did not believe, of course."

"Nay, I could not tell whether she believed it or not, but she only made light of it, I know. She said the sweet mother of mercy would never be hard upon a poor nun, since she was herself a woman, and that a few extra prayers and candles placed at her shrine would make up for any mistakes she might make. I wish I could tell her—dare tell her—that the mistake was in supposing that the Virgin could forgive her sins, and that these sins, which she thought so lightly of, had cost the Lord Christ His life. I wish I could tell every nun—every man and woman in St. Gilles—this wonderful story of Christ's love to men!"

"Hush! thou must be prudent, or Sister Ave and all who are suspected of believing this glorious truth will be sent to the cells underground. I have heard of such things being done here in this house."

"Well, I would endure imprisonment if that would make all the sisters embrace and believe this truth."

"But it would not—it would only deprive those whom we hope to influence of the opportunity of learning these things. There is that sad-looking stranger whom we each agreed to pray for last night. She may be glad to learn more of that which seemed to touch her so deeply; but how can she if Sister Ave and the rest of us are shut up in the dungeons under the crypt?"

"I will try to think of this and be prudent, but thou dost not know how hard it is to join in services that mean nothing to you, and see others putting their whole hope of salvation in the performance of a few penances, or lighting a few candles!"

And the warm-hearted girl burst into tears as she spoke.

Chapter XV

The Secret Meeting

ELFREDA, sitting on the other side of the leafy screen, could hear every word spoken by the two nuns; but to describe the mingled emotions that possessed her by turns would be impossible. She was grieved, shocked, and angry at the slighting way in which the intercession of the Virgin had been spoken of, and yet there was a deep joy in the thought that sinners might draw near the Lord Christ Himself; and she tried to accustom herself to the thought of this, but the force of habit was very strong, and she shrank from it at first, as being too bold and daring even to be thought of. Then she remembered what the nuns had said concerning herself, how they had noticed her sad looks and prayed for her, and she wished she could thank them for this, and ask them to read something more from the Scriptures.

But it did not seem likely that any opportunity would be afforded for this, for about midday they were summoned to the church, and after the service here they were marched to the refectory, where they were addressed by the superior, who bade them resume their works of piety and charity without delay; herself setting the example of industry by visiting each nun's cell, and confiscating all articles not conducive to their spiritual advancement.

The reason for this sudden change of policy soon became known. The pope's legate was expected to arrive shortly at Toulouse to inquire into the state of the Church, and to take such measures as were deemed needful for putting down this heresy of the Vaudois, or "good men."

Elfreda trembled when she heard the news—trembled for the fate of Sister Ave and her companions who held this dangerous doctrine, and she often looked at one or another of these as they went about among the other nuns, wondering how it was they could look so calm and undisturbed when they might at any hour be banished to the dungeons to await the coming of the legate, or be brought to trial at once before the bishop.

The secret of this calm peace and trust, Elfreda soon discovered, was not the result of indifference or defiance, as she was at first inclined to think, for on entering one of the corridors leading to the dormitories one day, she suddenly came upon Sister Ave, holding in her arms the young nun she had heard talking in the garden. The poor girl was in tears, and vainly trying to suppress them.

INDUSTRY: *diligence*

"Hush! hush!" whispered her companion. "'Let not your heart be troubled: ye believe in God, believe also in me.' Hast thou forgotten those words, little sister, and who spoke them?"

But the young nun had caught sight of Elfreda. "O, Sister Ave, we are discovered—betrayed!" she gasped.

Elfreda heard the words and instantly came forward. "Nay, do not fear me," she said; "I would not betray your secret even if I did not desire to learn more concerning this strange, good news. Wilt thou not teach me how to believe in the Lord Christ?" she suddenly asked.

Sister Ave looked at her keenly, for she had been told that the superior, following the example of the pope himself, had commanded some of the sisters to make inquisition among their companions, and secretly report to her all they could discover likely to prove that heresy was among them.

Elfreda did not know this, but she lifted her clear, truthful eyes, and looked so beseechingly at Sister Ave that she could not doubt the honesty of her request. "Dost thou know that the pope hath condemned this faith as heresy?" she asked.

Elfreda turned pale, and shivered at the sound of the dreadful word. "Why should it be heresy to believe in the Lord Christ, as the Scriptures command?" she ventured to ask.

But Sister Ave could only shake her head. "Evil men have made a gain of the ignorant, and this they would lose if men learned that Christ was waiting to receive them without penance and without payment. But I forget. The time I may have to talk to thee of these things is too precious to be wasted. Since thy soul is hungering for this knowledge thou wilt not care for the decrees of popes concerning it. Meet me in the garden after *vespers* and I will tell thee what I can, for we dare not bring forth our book from its hiding-place."

Sister Ave had most aptly expressed the feeling of Elfreda's soul. She was hungering after this knowledge of Christ with an intensity of longing that nothing else would satisfy. She had been some weeks in the convent now, and took her share with the other lay sisters in the more humble and arduous duties of the house; but whether she was engaged in these, or in prayer before the shrine of the Virgin, the thought, the desire that was ever springing up in her heart and mind was, "O that I could believe in the Lord Christ, as the Scriptures command!" In vain had she tried to reason down this longing by whispering the dread word heresy, and recalling the fact that it was for the suppression of this that the pope's legate had now come to Toulouse. He had even threatened Count Raymond with excommunication if he would not aid him in putting an end to the false doctrine. Papal decrees were all forgotten, and every objection silenced by the soul's longing cry for this knowledge, this rest, that Sister Ave and her companions seemed to enjoy.

ARDUOUS: *difficult*

And so as the shadows of evening closed round the quiet convent garden, Elfreda stole away from her companions and went to the spot agreed upon with Sister Ave. The faithful nun was there awaiting her, and bade her kneel down; and then, in a few simple words—words that carried Elfreda out of herself and seemed to place her at the very feet of the Lord Himself—she prayed for grace to speak the right words to this longing soul, and that Christ might be revealed to her as the Savior from all sin, and sorrow, and trouble.

Rising, she took Elfreda's hand, and they sat down in a little ruined alcove, and there, forgetting the lapse of time, she explained to the wondering girl the simple Gospel plan of salvation: how without works, without any merits of their own to recommend them to God's notice, men were invited to come, sin-stricken and sorrow-laden as they were, and for each and all Christ had the same words of invitation and welcome: "Come unto me, all ye that labor and are heavy laden, and I will give you rest. Take my yoke upon you, and learn of me; for I am meek and lowly in heart, and ye shall find rest unto your souls!"[1]

"O! I have labored, labored for years, to get rid of this load of sin and sorrow: the curse that seems to crush me with its weight!" exclaimed Elfreda, bursting into tears.

"And thou art still heavy laden in spite of all thy labor?" queried Sister Ave, tenderly.

"I thought the Church would lift this burden for

[1] MATTHEW 11:28-29

me if I only labored long enough, and laid up a store of good works."

"Poor child! thy hope hath been bitterly disappointed, I know, for the Church could never lift one sin from the soul of man. The Lord Christ alone can pardon, forgive, and bid thee rest."

"But how am I to come to Him?" burst forth Elfreda. "I would go on pilgrimage, or perform any penance, that I might come to Him as He bids us."

Sister Ave looked down at her silently, but with a tender, pitiful look in her eyes, and there was a slight tremor in her voice as she asked in a whisper, "Canst thou see me, Elfreda?"

"I cannot see the look of thy face, but I know thou art looking very pitiful," she said.

"Even so doth the Lord look upon thee, Elfreda, only more gently, more pityingly than I or any human friend can feel. He is as near thee, too, as I am, waiting for thee to come to Him now."

Elfreda started slightly at these words. "The holy Jesus here," she whispered, "and I—"

"Thou art full of sin, thou wouldst say. But be not afraid to draw near. Didst thou never hear the story of the thief on the cross?"

Some vague recollections of having read this in the old Saxon Bible flashed across Elfreda's mind, and she said quickly, "He pardoned the thief."

"Yes, He freely forgave him all his life-long sin when he asked that forgiveness."

"Only asking, only praying—will that truly be

enough?" asked Elfreda with trembling earnestness; and scarcely waiting for the nun's reply, she
fell upon her knees and sobbed forth, "O, Lord Jesus, I have been worse than the thief on the cross,
for I have a heavier curse to bear; but wilt thou
forgive me, and take this curse away, because—
because thou dost love and pity me, and died on
the cross to save me?"

Having once begun to pour out her heart in
prayer, Elfreda went on in disjointed sentences,
her voice broken with sobs, until Sister Ave began
to tremble for their safety; for should her companions miss her a search might be made, and they
might both get into trouble through it. So, with a
gentle whisper that it was time for them to go in-
doors, Sister Ave rose from her seat; but Elfreda
still continued her supplications. She rose, however, soon after the nun left her and managed to
overtake her before she entered the house.

"It is—it is true," she whispered. "The Lord Jesus
doth listen, and He hath helped me. O, Sister Ave,
I must go back to England and tell my aunt, and
all whom this curse resteth upon, that the Lord
Christ will help them to bear it."

It was hard to check Elfreda's outburst of joy,
but Sister Ave was obliged to warn her against dis-
closing this to anyone at St. Gilles. "I am suspected, and so are others of the sisters, so that thou
must be cautious, even in speaking to us, lest the
superior should suspect thee also; but I will tell thee

where thou canst learn more than I can teach thee concerning this good news. Thou art a lay sister, and art often in the marketplace; go there tomorrow at daybreak, and doubtless thou wilt find a little knot of people gathered round a preacher—he is a Vaudois pastor, a poor but holy man, who seeketh only the salvation of men's souls—pointing them to Christ, who hath died to redeem them. Join this little band, and, if thou canst do so, make thy way to the preacher afterward and tell him of any difficulties thou dost need to have explained, and thou mayest tell him Sister Ave sent thee."

Elfreda had only time to bid her friend a hasty farewell, when the door near which they were standing was quickly thrown open and a lay sister appeared.

She looked at Elfreda keenly and said, "I suppose I must pass over this trick of thine for once, but—well, I did not think *thou* wouldst have planned secret meetings in the garden, though some of the nuns have done it, I know, and the scandal hath been all hushed up. But thou hadst better not follow in the ways of Sister Ave and one or two others I could name, for they have listened in the marketplace to these Vaudois preachers—these 'good men'—who are trying to upset the Church and turn the world upside down."

"Are they?" uttered Elfreda mechanically, not knowing what else to say; and, fearing she might betray something of her secret, she hastened to-

SUNDRY: *various*

ward the kitchen, where she had some duties to perform before retiring to rest.

The next morning she was at the marketplace making sundry purchases that were needed, and carefully looking for the little crowd of people that would denote where the preacher had taken his stand; but it was only after a careful search that she discovered the little gathering, for they were screened from general observation by a projecting portico, and evidently had no wish to court further publicity.

As Elfreda crept into a vacant corner where she could not only hear the preacher, but see his pale, earnest face, without being herself noticed, he was uttering these words: "Our enemies accuse us of teaching newfangled notions, which no bishop of the Church hath ever professed or taught; but this, my friends, is false, for I will read from this parchment the words of Claude, Bishop of Turin, who wrote four hundred years ago, not long after the famous Council of Frankfort, where the pope's legates were plainly told that it was unlawful to worship images. Claude in this letter saith:

"'It deserves to be well-considered that if men ought not to adore and serve the works of God's hands, there is much stronger reason for not adoring or serving the works of men's hands, not even with the adoration due to those whom it is pretended they represent; for if the image you adore

DENOTE: *mark*
PORTICO: *a covered porch*
COURT: *gain*

is not God, you ought by no means to adore it
with the adoration offered to saints, who make
no pretension to divine honors. We ought, then,
carefully to bear this in mind—that all those who
pay divine honors not only to visible images, but
to any creature, whether celestial or terrestrial,
spiritual or corporeal, and who expect from it the
salvation which comes from God alone, are of that
class whom the apostle describes as "serving the
creature more than the Creator."[1] Return, blind
mortals, to your light! Return to Him who "light-
eth every man that cometh into the world!"[2] This
"Light shineth in darkness, and the darkness com-
prehendeth it not."[3] Hearken everyone of you who,
not seeing or not regarding the light, walk in darkness, and know not whither you go, because that
darkness hath blinded your eyes! Foolish men,
who, by going to Rome, seek the intercession of
the apostle, hear what St. Augustine saith: "Come
with me, and consider why we love the apostles. Is
it on account of their human nature? Is it because
we believe they were men? No, certainly, for then
we should no longer have anything to love, since
the man exists no longer; his soul hath quitted his
body. But we believe that what we love in him still
lives. If the believer must believe God when He
promises, how much more when he swears, and
says, 'Though Noah, Daniel, and Job were in that
town'[4]—that is to say, if the saints whom you in-
voke were filled with a sanctity, a righteousness, a

[1]ROMANS 1:25 [2]JOHN 1:9 [3]JOHN 1:5 [4]EZEKIEL 14:20
CELESTIAL OR TERRESTRIAL: *heavenly or earthly*
CORPOREAL: *physical*

The Vaudois Preacher

merit, as great as those persons possessed—'they should deliver neither son nor daughter?'[1] And for this purpose he hath declared that no one may put confidence in either the merits or the intercession of saints, since if he himself doth not persevere in the faith, in the righteousness and truth, in which they persevered, and by which they pleased God, he cannot be saved." Be converted, ye prevaricators, who have withdrawn yourselves from the truth, who crucify the Son of God afresh, and expose Him to open shame. God commands one thing, and these people do another. God commands to bear the cross, not to adore it; these persons adore it, while they bear it neither corporeally nor spiritually.'

"Brethren, these are the words of a bishop of holy and blameless life. Consider, therefore, whether these things which we teach, and the pope's legate hath come hither to suppress, are evil, newfangled, and against the warrant of Scripture and clerkly learning. Consider, I pray ye, and choose whom ye will serve and adore—the Lord Jesus Christ, or the cross on which He died; the Lord Christ, or His followers, who can save neither son nor daughter; the Lord Christ, or the work of men's hands—graven images upon which you can see the workman use his tools. 'Choose this day whom ye will serve.'"[2]

[1] EZEKIEL 14:20   [2] JOSHUA 24:15

PREVARICATORS: *liars*

Chapter XVI

Domínic de Guzman

THE streets of St. Gilles were filled with a motley crowd. Scholars from the academies, for which the South of France was already beginning to grow famous; sculptors and painters, who had just run out of their studios; merchants and shopkeepers, priests and monks; troubadours, trilling their satirical songs in the ears of their clerical neighbors, and keeping a sharp lookout for any fresh incident that might give spice and sparkle to their next popular lay;—these, and many others, thronged the avenues to witness the great procession which had been ordered by the new papal legate, Peter Castelnau. And truly it was a great procession—a gorgeous display, in which every church in St. Gilles was represented.

The predecessor of this legate had returned to Rome with the information that Count Raymond and all Languedoc were thoroughly impracticable. The cities were possessed of a liberty un-

PREDECESSOR: *one who held the position before him*
IMPRACTICABLE: *difficult, stubborn*
IMPLICIT: *unquestioning*
DOGMAS: *established beliefs*

known in the north. Their language, so rich and flexible, had been abundantly cultivated in both prose and verse; and to be a man of learning, or a poet of elegance, was to gain a footing at once in the court. Priests and monks had watched the progress of this love of letters with anxiety, and had tried to check it; for it was very evident that a people who had advanced to this stage would not long listen with implicit faith to the dogmas of the Church. Indeed, already there was manifested a love of liberty in religion, as well as civil matters, which provoked the utmost rancor on the part of the ecclesiastical authorities.

Finding, however, their efforts to check the progress of learning vain, these Churchmen sought to neutralize its effects, especially in religious matters, by fostering by their example the love of pleasure—of vicious indulgence, indeed, in some instances. This, as we have seen, served its purpose with the great majority—the frivolous and the gay. But the more serious and devout were only thus the more estranged from the Church and its ministers, and they gladly turned to the Vaudois, or "poor men," who, making no pretense of peculiar sanctity, lived so purely and blamelessly that the hearts of those who disapproved of their doctrines were won by their blameless lives.

It was to impress these wanderers from the Church with its power and majesty that the present

RANCOR: *hatred*
ECCLESIASTICAL: *Church*
VICIOUS INDULGENCE: *evil indulgence*
PECULIAR SANCTITY: *exceptional holiness*

"progress" of the legate and other great dignitaries was undertaken. And certainly, if pomp and splendor, gorgeous vestments and sacred relics, could impress with religious fervor the hearts of men, these people of Languedoc should at once have become devout, and forever have forgotten the poor, shabby Vaudois. Doubtless Castelnau, burning with anger against these daring innovators, cast sidelong but anxious glances at the crowd that lined every street; but he certainly could have seen nothing beyond gaping curiosity or smiles of ridicule, and perhaps occasionally a cold sneer or a satirical song penetrated his ears.

Among those gathered near the gate of St. Gilles was a young Spaniard named Dominic de Guzman. His grave, earnest soul had been greatly shocked during his stay in Languedoc, not only by the lightness of the people, but also by the progress these new doctrines had made. He saw that such a processional display as this would prove worse than fruitless, and, full of devout plans, he sought an early interview with the legate himself.

"Men can never be won by such a display as this," he said with emphasis. "See you not how you strengthen the cause of these heretics? They are poor and earnest, and ask nothing but food and raiment of their followers. Take a lesson from them. Cast away these trinkets and gauds, and go barefoot through the streets, preaching every-

PROGRESS: *procession*
VESTMENTS: *robes*
GAUDS: *ornaments*

where the power and mercy of our blessed Lady, even as I myself will do."

Everybody was astonished, but, of course, the bishops declined to lay aside their wealth and dignity. Only one or two of those who heard Dominic were impressed by the holy fervor that shone in his earnest face, and promised to join him in his novel crusade against the Vaudois heretics. At the same time the legate exhorted all the bishops to make diligent inquisition for those holding these evil doctrines, that they might in due time be handed over to the secular power for punishment. He also declared that Count Raymond must be compelled to deal with his subjects as the pope directed, regardless of his own opinions in the matter.

So Dominic and his two or three companions, laying aside all their distinctions of rank, clothed themselves in shabby and ragged garments, bound around their waists by a rope, and went barefoot through the streets, preaching in the marketplaces wherever a crowd could be collected, and begging their meals at the doors of the poorer houses.

These preaching mendicant friars caused far more sensation than the recent exhibition of churchly pomp and magnificence, and multitudes listened with rapt attention to Dominic's burning words of eloquent appeal and marveled greatly. What new thing, thought they, will the world see next, now that men in the Church, as well as heretics, show themselves anxious to save other souls

NOVEL: *new*
MENDICANT FRIARS: *monks who supported themselves by begging*

than their own? It soon came to be understood that Dominic would found a new brotherhood of monks, and would gladly receive any who, instead of devoting themselves to a life of contemplation within the walls of a monastery, were willing to go through the world teaching and preaching, and seeking to bring men into the Church.

It was a great reformation Dominic sought to bring about—a great step in advance of all the other monastic orders—but he did not preach Christ and His salvation. The holiness and greatness of the Church, and the merits and intercessory work of the Virgin Mary, were the subjects of his sermons; and, to aid his followers in their devotions, he invented what was called the "Rosary of the Most Blessed Virgin."

This rosary was a string of beads containing fifteen large ones, which were known as "Paternosters," or prayers to God, and one hundred and fifty smaller ones, called "Ave Marias," or prayers to the Virgin. That these soon became very popular with the easy-going, pleasure-loving people of Languedoc is easy to imagine, for by just passing these beads through their fingers a hundred and sixty-five prayers were set down to their account; and this was part of the "good works" that Dominic enjoined.

Meanwhile Elfreda went to listen to the Vaudois preaching, as well as to hear the young Spaniard. This latter she was commanded to do by the supe-

ENJOINED: *ordered*

rior, but Dominic's words made little impression upon her now.

"Christ is in my heart, teaching me by His Holy Spirit, so that I am not likely to seek Mary to intercede for me with Him," she said one day when Sister Ave had thought it needful to whisper a few words of caution about the use of the new rosary which had lately been given to the nuns.

The Church was everywhere upholding these new preaching friars, and rousing a spirit of persecution against those who believed the simple truth of the Gospel instead of the dogmas of the Church; and Count Raymond was at last threatened that if he showed no more respect for the rights of Church property and lands than he did for those of his subjects, and did not punish and imprison those whom the bishops accused of heresy, his country should be invaded by a foreign foe, and given over to his enemies as a reward for their devotion to the Church.

Count Raymond smiled at the threat as an extravagant one, and politely told the legate that in time of war the Church lands could not always be exempt from invasion, and that the "poor men" and Vaudois among his subjects should not be imprisoned except for breaking the laws of the State, even at the bidding of Pope Innocent.

The legate was angry, and so was the pope; but the people of Toulouse were more indignant than either at this threatened invasion of their liberties,

EXTRAVAGANT: *excessive*

and some foolishly thought that if this fanatical legate could only be got rid of, the whole business would be settled, and the persecution of the Vaudois and "poor men" would be at an end. In an evil hour someone resolved to rid Count Raymond of this enemy, and as the legate and a party of priests and attendants were crossing the river at St. Gilles, a lance was aimed at him so surely that it passed through his body, causing almost instant death.

To describe the consternation that prevailed in the town when this foul deed was made known would be impossible. The priests and monks threatened the utmost vengeance of Heaven against the whole land for this murder of one whose person was sacred—who was the representative of the pope himself—God's vicar and vicegerent. Dominic spoke of it as putting God to death, and directly accused Count Raymond of having instigated the murder; and this tale was carried to Rome, where the pope, to serve his own purposes, was only too ready to believe it. He consequently issued his edict, laying the ban of the Church on all who should hold friendly intercourse with the offender or his people, and denying to them all the rites, ceremonies, and comforts of religion. In addition to this he called upon all true Christian warriors to bind themselves in a holy crusade against Raymond. His appeal closed thus:

VICAR: *representative*
VICEGERENT: *lieutenant*

"Count Raymond of Toulouse has murdered the pope's legate. Up, defenders of the cross, and enter upon a holy crusade against this heresy which threatens to destroy the Church in the south of France! Up, and fight for the defense of holy mother Church, and the lands and possessions of the heretics shall be the lawful spoil of those who engage in this holy warfare!"

This was the cry sent through Europe by command of the pope. Bishops and priests exhorted their flocks to join this new crusade, and there were plenty found who needed little urging to engage in a war that promised such rich and easily gained spoil as the wealth of Languedoc.

Simon de Montfort was chosen leader of this crusade, as he had been of the last, and under such a devoted leader many of the archbishops in the north of France girded on coats of mail beneath the gorgeous robes that were intended to proclaim them as the servants of the Prince of Peace.

Count Raymond had smiled when his kingdom was laid under an interdict, for he knew that it would make little difference to his flourishing commerce. Many others of his subjects, besides the Vaudois, had openly revolted from the Church, and those who still remained within her pale cared so little for her commands, that they would not becloud their commercial prospects

INTERDICT: *a formal order forbidding participation in the services of the church*
PALE: *bounds*

by refusing to buy or sell with their neighbors. A few priests refused to open the churches for divine service, or perform any of the rites of the Church; but there were others who were quite as willing to baptize, marry, and bury their parishioners, as they were to buy and sell in defiance of the pope's command.

A few of the Vaudois left Toulouse, and returned to their native valleys of the Alps; but most of those who had been chosen pastors, teachers, and missionaries, remained faithfully at their posts, although they knew that complaints had been made against them. The Inquisition, as a special tribunal, had not yet been heard of, but the abominable method lately adopted, of making secret inquiry for the discovery of heretics, was its commencement; and who more fitting to carry out its designs— the crushing of heresy—than these new mendicant friars, who, under the direction of Dominic, were now preaching in every town of Languedoc? Many who were unable to preach could go from house to house, begging, and watching the movements of different individuals. Thus were wormed out the secrets of families, and information was lodged against many who thought themselves unsuspected.

So the weeks and months glided on until the legate had been dead a year, and then, as the spring began to open, came tidings of the new crusade that was gathering its forces in the north.

WORMED OUT: *slyly found out*

England, Normandy, and France, would each con-
tribute its quota to avenge the terrible insult and
wrong against the holy father by the murder of his
messenger and representative. The interdict might
be laughed at, but an invading army was too real
and tangible a foe to be sneered off his borders,
so Count Raymond began to make overtures of
peace to his master at Rome.

Nothing but the most abject humiliation of the
refractory count would satisfy Pope Innocent, and
he was summoned to appear at Valence, and there
condemned to walk, stripped to the waist, to the
abbey church, holding a lighted candle, and after
doing penance at the altar was led to the tomb of
the murdered legate.

Such humble submission to the pope would
surely be sufficient to disarm all his hostility, and
secure the withdrawal of the troops now gathering at Lyons. Count Raymond most certainly felt
sure of this, or so proud a knight would never have
submitted to such degradation; and Pope Innocent may have intended to turn back the "crusaders" from their work of destruction. But he had
raised a power he was unable to control. Priests
and monks had not only promised escape from
purgatory and plenary indulgence for all sin to
those who joined this war against heresy, but, what
was far more tempting to most of the soldiers and
adventurers who formed this vast host, the wealth
of prosperous towns like Beziers and Toulouse was

REFRACTORY: *stubbornly disobedient*
PLENARY INDULGENCE: *complete forgiveness*

promised them as lawful spoil; and their passions of avarice and ambition were more easily aroused than quelled.

It was on June 18, 1209, that Count Raymond performed his degrading penance in the abbey church of Valence, and in less than a month Simon de Montfort, with the archbishops of Rheims, Sens, and Rouen, had marched their horde of semi-barbarians into the rich plains of Languedoc. Montpelier soon fell before the invading host, and about the end of July Beziers fell into their hands after a short resistance. It was an awful scene—a sight to make angels weep—these archbishops, with a train of priests chanting hymns of praise to God, leading savage and bloodthirsty men to slaughter their fellowmen because they dared to worship God with a purer, simpler worship.

Was it possible that men like De Montfort, who, with all his ambition, was yet a brave, true-hearted knight, and not a monster—or others, like the gentle, devout, enthusiastic Dominic de Guzman—was it possible that they could believe they were doing God service when, with their consent, seven thousand innocent and unarmed people who had taken sanctuary in and around the church of St. Mary Magdalene in this town of Beziers were basely butchered? It is said that one of the archbishops ordered this massacre, and on being reminded that some were Catholics, he coolly said, "Kill them all! God will know His own." Ah, truly,

AVARICE: *greed*
QUELLED: *quieted*
CLEMENCY: *mercy*

"precious in the sight of the Lord is the death of his saints."[1] Nothing but the utter extermination of the heretics and despoiling of Languedoc would satisfy the crusaders or their priestly leaders, and that they did not fully succeed was by no means owing to their clemency, for a more unjust and cruel war was never waged against any people. While reading this dark page of the world's history we need to keep fast hold of our faith, that—

> "The great world's altar stairs
> Slope through darkness up to God,"[2]

or we should be utterly bewildered. But we can by its means confidently trust, knowing that "God is light, and in him is no darkness at all."[3]

---

[1] PSALM 116:15
[2] *In Memoriam,* by Lord Alfred Tennyson
[3] I JOHN 1:5

Chapter XVII

At Beziers

THE superior of the convent to which Elfreda belonged was not at all anxious for the bishop to be apprised of the heretical proclivities of any under her charge, for it might be that she herself would be called to account. She knew that numerous scandals already afloat had caused some questioning as to the wisdom of her rule and her fitness for the position. All sorts of inquiries had been made and suspicions fostered since these heretics had brought their nation to the notice of the holy father. And now Dominic de Guzman publicly criticized the nuns and monks, and in eloquent words exhorted them to reform their rule, and live as pure and simple lives as those foes of the Church, the Vaudois. "Just as though implicit belief in the doctrine of the mother Church was not better than mere purity of morals," sighed the lady superior. "These are degenerate days," and as she concluded her reflection she sent for Elfreda to come to her private apartment.

APPRISED: *informed*
PROCLIVITIES: *tendencies*

It was not often that a lay sister was admitted to the presence of the superior, and Elfreda trembled a little as she walked along the corridor. She had been warned by Sister Ave the day before that she was suspected of heresy, and that it might be that she was now to be accused of it. But Elfreda need have had little fear. The superior hated trouble, and would have considered a lay sister too insignif- icant an individual to be formally accused of her- esy. She had, however, been informed of her visits to the place where the "poor men" and Vaudois met for prayer, and so she had decided to get rid of her without delay. It was not difficult to do this in the case of a lay sister, and so an hour later Elf- reda was walking along the road toward Toulouse, whither she had been abruptly transferred by the superior's orders.

It grieved Elfreda much to leave St. Gilles with- out a word of farewell to Sister Ave or her Christian friends in the town; but the superior's order had been imperative—she must leave without delay. The letter she was to take was already written, and with this in her hand she was sent out to seek a new home. What excuse had been made in it for her abrupt dismissal Elfreda did not know; but when she presented it at the convent at Toulouse she was told, rather abruptly, that no lay sisters could be received there, and that she had better return to St. Gilles. This, however, Elfreda was not disposed to do. Sister Ave had urged her to leave while she

IMPERATIVE: *commanding*

had the opportunity, but she had shrunk from cutting herself off entirely from a monastic life; and her work among the sick and poor often gave her an opportunity of pointing the weary, heavy-laden sufferers directly to the great burden-bearer—to Him who hath "borne our griefs and carried our sorrows,"[1]—instead of urging them to perform penance or seek the aid of the saints.

Now, however, it seemed that God in His providence had thrust her out into the world, and she must perforce look elsewhere for shelter and employment. She knew there were "poor men" at Toulouse, and so after leaving the convent she made her way to the marketplace, where she hoped to find some of them preaching.

She soon saw a dense crowd gathered around the great stone cross in the center, but she well-knew that Vaudois barbs would not choose such a central position as that. As she drew nearer she saw that it was the young Spaniard, Dominic, who was pleading with the crowd, beseeching them in earnest and impassioned tones to turn away from false heretical teachers, who would deprive them of all the benefits and comforts the Church could afford, and at last rob them of heaven itself.

"The blessed Mary, ever virgin, hath sent me to plead with you, her willful children. The gracious queen of heaven is in grief because ye neglect her worship and follow these evil men. Will ye not listen to her gracious pleadings when she,

[1] Isaiah 53:4
PROVIDENCE: *all-seeing care and direction*
PERFORCE: *be forced by circumstances to*

the ever merciful, bids you return to the bosom of the Church? Will ye utterly despise her mercy, and bring down the wrath of Heaven upon this land?"

So Dominic pleaded, and none who heard him could doubt his earnest love for the souls he believed to be in danger of destruction.

Elfreda sighed as she turned away. "O that the Church could be reformed, could be taught to see that the Lord Christ, and not His mother, is the only hope set forth for guilty man! and that a blessing and not a curse follows upon casting the soul upon Him for salvation;" and for a moment a smile flitted over her face, but it was as quickly succeeded by another sigh. "O, that Guy could learn this glorious truth—the truth that has set me free from that dreadful bondage of fear and dread in which I lived so long, and which I know hath shadowed all his life as well!"

Thus thinking, Elfreda had reached a little, quiet nook, where, as she expected, a Vaudois pastor had a few devoted listeners gathered around him. She mingled with the little company, and when the preaching was over, and they had dispersed, she spoke to the pastor—telling him her circumstances, and asking to be directed to a decent home.

"I am not penniless," she said, for she had made up her mind to apply to old Nathan for some of that store of zechins he had spoken of; but she did not wish to take up her abode with the Jews again,

BARBS: *preachers*

and so thought to secure a home first before applying to Nathan for money.

The minister smiled as she explained this to him. "I see thou knowest we have little of this world's wealth. But we have always a store for strangers, and to a share of that thou art welcome, as well as to a shelter beneath our roof," he added. He then proposed to take Elfreda at once to the house of a widow in the outskirts of the town, where she could stay for the night, at least, for the shadows of evening were drawing near, and the gay capital of Languedoc was no safe place for an unprotected woman after nightfall.

So Elfreda agreed to postpone her visit to old Nathan until the following day, and went at once to the widow's house. It was a day ever to be remembered in Elfreda's life—the day in which the last tie that bound her to the Church of Rome was riven asunder, and the quiet, solemn gladness of the evening spent in this widow's house was a fitting close to it.

As the minister had said, the Vaudois were for the most part a poor people, for, though protected by the powerful Count Raymond, they did not engage in trade either as small chapmen or large merchants, but were for the most part simple artisans, working industriously at their trades, but so scrupulously honest, both as to the character of the work done and the amount of payment demanded, that they could barely supply the wants

RIVEN ASUNDER: *torn apart*
CHAPMEN: *tradesmen*
ARTISANS: *craftsmen*

of their families, and so had little to spare for the purchase of books. In consequence, a common fund, to which all contributed a trifle, had long since been formed, and by this means the Scriptures—all the New Testament and several of the books of the Old—had been purchased, a portion at a time, and each evening they met at some one of their houses, where the schoolmaster or pastor would read a chapter from the Word of God, which would then be discussed by all present, and in this way even children—for many of them came with their parents—gained an intimate knowledge of the Word of God, which was their surest protection against being drawn aside from the faith by such specious arguments as those of Dominic and his mendicant friars.

This evening the meeting was to be held at the house of Elfreda's host, and when they were all assembled—mothers and fathers bringing their children—it seemed like some happy, social, family gathering; and more like heaven than any convent she had ever seen, Elfreda thought.

The next day she went to see her Jewish friends, and there heard, to her great disappointment, that old Nathan had removed from Toulouse to Beziers. There she resolved to follow him, intending to return to Toulouse as soon as her business with him was settled.

On reaching old Nathan's house she was told that he was very ill—too ill to leave his room or

SPECIOUS: *deceptively pleasing*

receive strangers—and it was only after begging his servant very earnestly to tell the old man that Elfreda, from England, wished to see him, that anyone would consent to let him know she had come. As soon as her message was delivered, however, she was summoned to the sick man's room, and old Nathan's first words prevented her from thinking of returning to Toulouse.

"The Lord God of my fathers hath verily heard my prayer, and sent thee to comfort the soul of His servant ere he die. Elfreda, thou wilt not leave me again—thou wilt not leave the old man among strangers, for dear as a daughter hast thou been to me since the time when thou didst show favor and kindness to the Jew."

The rapid, earnest utterance of the old man had almost exhausted him, and he fell back upon the pile of cushions upon which he was reclining as though each labored breath he drew would be the last. Elfreda was surprised to see such a change in him. "I am very sorry," she said, looking pityingly at the sallow, withered face, which seemed the more ghastly because of its contrast with the crimson satin cushion on which his head rested.

"I am a poor old man—very poor, very poor," he panted, slowly opening his eyes and looking round at the richly-embroidered arras, gold candlesticks, and jeweled cups that stood near him. The room was furnished with oriental splendor and magnificence, and Elfreda wondered what old Nathan

SALLOW: *sickly, yellowish*

could mean, for he did not speak in his usual whining tone of cringing servility, but as though he was communing with himself.

"Can I do anything for thee?" Elfreda asked after a pause.

"Thou wilt stay, Elfreda—thou wilt stay with me," gasped the old man.

"Yes, I will stay," said Elfreda.

"Now the God of Abraham, Isaac, and Israel bless thee for that word, my daughter. He will bless Elfreda," said the old man emphatically.

"He hath blessed me," responded Elfreda quietly.

Old Nathan looked up in her face.

"Thou art changed, Elfreda—thou dost look like one at rest, instead of being storm-tossed and beaten down by this world's trials. Is there a haven of rest in this world?"

"Yes, I have been storm-tossed, but I have found the rest and peace the Church promised but could not give. I have found it in Christ Jesus the Lord."

"The Nazarene again—always the Church or the Nazarene," muttered old Nathan. But in a minute or two he turned again to Elfreda and said gently, "Sit down, and tell me about this haven of rest. I had thought I would be happy—would find peace and joy—in the possession of gold and silver and precious stones; but I have gathered these to me in vain, for this day I feel poor—I am a poor, lonely, loveless old man, with none to care whether I live or die. Yes, I am very poor," he added.

"But God can enrich thee," said Elfreda. "He can give thee what thy gold cannot buy—the knowledge and love of Himself."

"But thy God is not my God," said old Nathan.

"Nay, but He is," replied Elfreda. "I believe in the God of Abraham, Isaac, and Israel—believe that He loved me so much that He gave His Son, the Lord Jesus Christ, to die for me, that my sins might be pardoned, that all my foolish, proud, willful thoughts and deeds might be forgiven, and the guilt of them washed away in the precious blood of Christ."

"But we are His chosen people, and believe not in this Nazarene," said old Nathan.

"But ye believe that, chosen as ye are, ye have sinned?" said Elfreda.

"Sinned! Aye, most grievously have we and our fathers sinned against the law of our God. Therefore are we banished from our goodly land, and compelled to bear the heavy curse of His wrath."

"I had to bear such a curse once, or thought I had, but I have learned now that the Lord Christ hath taken it away; that He bore the curse of our sins, and that there remaineth naught but blessing for us if we will only believe in His love and accept it."

"Nay, nay, but my Scripture saith the curse of the fathers shall be visited on the children," said Nathan.

"And the Scripture also saith that the Lord delighteth in mercy," replied Elfreda. "Shall I tell thee of the curse of the Ericsons—the curse that hath shadowed all my life, and that of Guy de Valery, too?"

The old man was almost as pleased as a child at the prospect of hearing a story, and eagerly assented. So, in as few words as possible, that she might not weary him, Elfreda told the story of the heretic monk of Crowland, and how the Church had held its terrible ban over the heads of her family, doubtless as a warning against future heresy; and how she had lately discovered that, after all, there was no curse, but the evil things which she had supposed were its results had come in the most natural order; and how the knowledge this old monk had gained in the Vaudois valley was the same knowledge of God and His love to men which she had lately learned.

"And Guy de Valery, hath he learned the secret of this peace?" asked Nathan.

Elfreda shook her head, and turned aside to hide her emotion. "I would to God I could find him to tell him of this," she said.

"Peradventure thou wilt find him if thou dost return to England; but tarry awhile, my daughter, until I am laid in the grave, and then thou shalt go back a rich lady, for thy zechins have multiplied in my hands, and I will restore them fourfold."

Elfreda did not need this to induce her to stay

ASSENTED: *agreed*
PERADVENTURE: *perhaps*

with old Nathan. She could see that the old man
had greatly changed, and she felt it to be her duty
to devote herself to him for the few remaining
weeks or months of his life. It might be that, in
spite of his prejudice against the Christian faith,
she might yet lead him to look to the Lord Jesus
for pardon and salvation; and this hope made her
forget the tedium of a sick-room, and the disgrace,
as many would deem it, of associating with Jews.

And so the weeks and months glided on, until
at last the tidings came of the crusade that the
Church had organized against heresy; even now it
was marching toward Languedoc.

"If thy God delighted in loving and blessing, this
Church, that professeth to follow Him, glorieth in
hating and cursing. The curse of Languedoc for
her heresy will be no imaginary curse, like that
of thy family, Elfreda, for the bloodhounds of war
are let loose to consume this heresy; and may God
defend His own when Simon de Montfort fighteth
against them!"

The old Jew roused himself once more to secure
his wealth from falling into the hands of the invaders, and then begged Elfreda to leave him while
yet there was time for her to escape to England.

But this she positively refused to do. She would
stay with him to the end, and this she did; but the
gates of Beziers were closed the very day old Nathan died.

Chapter XVIII

An Unexpected Meeting

THE house where old Nathan lived was near the middle of the town, and Elfreda heard only the distant roar of the contending armies; but the numerous parties of fugitives who took refuge in the great church of St. Mary Magdalene soon convinced the most hopeful that the besiegers were rapidly gaining advantage after advantage, and that the town would soon be in the hands of De Montfort's host.

Old Nathan had expected some of his friends from Toulouse to attend his funeral, but no one had been able to come. The Jews of Beziers, however, had seen that the last rites were performed according to their kinsman's wish; and then one of them, pitying Elfreda's helpless condition, and knowing that she would receive no sympathy from their Catholic neighbors, went to the castle, and begged a refuge for her there under the protection of Count Raymond's sister, who was well-known to favor the Vaudois, or "poor men," if indeed she had not entirely embraced their faith.

So when the crowds of refugees going to the Church of St. Mary became more frequent, Elfreda resolved to avail herself of the refuge offered her in the castle, and, to her great joy, she found there several of the Vaudois pastors, besides many noble ladies who had refused to leave their homes and seek safety in flight while there were so many poor and helpless still in town whom they could perhaps protect.

Here the noise of the catapults and other engines of war could be plainly heard, as well as the shrieks of the wounded and the groans of the dying; and many a poor wounded creature was brought in to have his wounds tended by gentler hands than those of the rough soldiery outside.

Nor was De Montfort unmindful of the wounded among his men. A party of Knights Hospitalers were frequently to be seen moving about among the wounded, soothing their last moments, or doing what they could to relieve their sufferings. It sometimes happened that one of these, on his mission of mercy, would come close up to the castle gates—passing through the terrible breaches in the wall almost unheeded, for the white cross on their mantles insured them against the arrows of the archers or the thrusts of the javelin men, and it was rarely that one of these soldier monks was wounded.

It was the fifth day of the siege, the day after

Elfreda had reached the castle, when one of the ladies, peeping through a loophole of the castle to note the progress of the enemy, saw a Knight Hospitaler struck down by an arrow, and lying unconscious, and apparently unnoticed, by either friend or foe.

"'Tis a right brave knight, and a merciful, albeit he is one of our enemies," said the Lady of Beziers, and she directed a party of her retainers to go out by the secret subterranean door and bring the knight into the castle. This was speedily done, and Elfreda, having had great experience in nursing and dressing of wounds, was directed to have all things in readiness for him in a little alcove near the lady's bower. Ladies, and guests, and bower-maidens were all pressed into the service of nursing, and there were few idle hands in the castle now that could be made useful.

For herself, Elfreda had little hope of escape from death now, but it was a great relief to be in the castle, under the protection of the brave count and his retainers; here they might hope to die without being exposed to the brutality of the rough soldiery, and this seemed an unspeakable mercy. But the prospect of death had little terror for Elfreda now. There was no fearful purgatory darkening with its grim shadow all the future life. She knew that death would be but the beginning of life to her, and yet—yet she often sighed as she thought of the far off English castle and her

LOOPHOLE: *narrow window*
SUBTERRANEAN: *underground*
UNSPEAKABLE: *incredible*

Cousin Guy. If she might but see him once more, and tell him they had been making a terrible mistake all this time; that God had not cursed, but blessed, the old monk, Leofwine, and that he had given them a blessing, not a curse, in the gift of that old Saxon Bible—the family heirloom! But, alas! what hope was there now of her ever seeing England, or Guy either. She was indulging in a reverie like this when summoned to attend the wounded Knight Hospitaler, and in making the needful arrangements for his reception everything else was forgotten.

Elfreda scarcely glanced at the face of the soldier while assisting to remove his mantle and armor, and it was not until his wound was dressed, and the leech had withdrawn to attend another of his patients, that Elfreda had time to look at the pale countenance before her. She started and trembled, but still with only a half-recognition, until the wounded man slowly opened his eyes on momentarily regaining consciousness, and then in an instant she knew him—knew, in spite of the aged, worn appearance, it was no other than her Cousin Guy. It seemed, however, that there was little likelihood of his ever recognizing her, or being able to listen to the glad tidings she longed to impart, for day after day passed and he made no visible progress toward recovery. The town capitulated, and, of course, the castle surrendered; but Guy still lay in semi-unconsciousness, faithfully attended by Elfreda.

CAPITULATED: *surrendered*

When the castle was taken, and free exit was allowed to all who chose to depart, several tried to persuade Elfreda to leave the knight to the care of the victors, telling her the castle was no place for a woman now; but Elfreda would not leave her cousin's side, and De Montfort was only too glad that a follower who was so faithful and devout a Catholic as De Valery should have the benefit of her care. So the lady's bower remained as sacred a spot as it had been when the Lady of Beziers had occupied it.

Of the progress of the terrible crusade Elfreda heard but little; but it went mercilessly on. Town after town submitted to the conquerors; and all through that awful summer, while the sun was smiling upon the earth, coloring its flowers and ripening its fruits, hordes of savage soldiery were marching through beautiful Languedoc, trampling down the maize, burning farmhouses, rooting up vineyards, and killing all who fell into their hands. Sometimes a whisper of these atrocities would reach Elfreda, but days often passed when she would hear nothing but the tramp of armed men as they passed her door, or exchanged a few words with the attendant who brought her food.

At length, however, this dreary monotony was broken, and Elfreda's fainting heart was cheered by her patient asking, in a feeble but natural voice, what the day was. For a moment Elfreda had forgotten, but she answered, as calmly and quickly as she could, "Wednesday."

ATROCITIES: *horrible cruelties*

"Nay, but which saint is it sacred to?" asked the knight.

Elfreda shook her head. She had forgotten to keep account of the saint's days lately, and she frankly confessed it.

"Then thou art one of these miserable Vaudois whom holy Church hath seen good to chastise," said the knight, crossing himself as a defense against heretic spells.

Again Elfreda bowed, for she was afraid to trust her voice.

Guy looked at her curiously, but only sighed, as, after the scrutiny, he turned his head away, and Elfreda went to prepare him some nourishing food. When she brought it, and prepared to feed him, as usual, he quietly submitted to all she chose to do, watching her with eager, curious eyes. He did not speak until the meal was concluded, and then he said:

"Doth the noble Count de Montfort, or any other in this castle, know thou art an accursed heretic?"

Again Elfreda shook her head.

"Then I will not betray thy secret, although it may be that it is a deadly sin to conceal such foul heresy as thine."

Elfreda looked troubled, and scarcely knew how to repress the words that came rushing to her lips; but she knew that the least agitation might endanger her cousin's life, and for his sake she carefully concealed every sign of emotion as she carried away the platter, and silver cup from which he had drunk a little wine.

"So like, so like her, and yet so hardened a heretic," murmured Guy, half-aloud, as Elfreda withdrew.

What would he have said could he have followed her, and seen how she threw herself on the floor, burying her face in a cushion that her sobs might not be heard; or could he have seen her afterward when, somewhat calmed, she slowly rose and fell on her knees to pour out her heart before God in prayer on his behalf. But Guy knew nothing of all this, and so let his thoughts wander back to that time when he lay sick at the Jew's house in London, until he fell into a refreshing sleep.

When he awoke it was to notice that in the room where he lay there was neither cross nor crucifix —nothing to which he could turn as he prayed; and it seemed to him that without these external helps his prayer could never rise even to the merciful Virgin mother or the saints, and it was a great blessing he wished to ask—one that only God Himself could grant. He did not believe that any saint was powerful enough to turn the heart of a heretic Vaudois; and it was for the conversion of his kind and tender nurse, who so strongly reminded him of his Cousin Elfreda, that he prayed, although he feared it would be quite unavailing of itself.

By and by Elfreda came in again, bringing some medicine, and looking so calm and placid that Guy was instinctively reminded of the sweet, calm face of the Madonna he had seen in some of the churches. Try as he would, he could not keep his eyes from watching her, until at last he startled her out of her calmness and composure by exclaiming, "It is—*it is* Elfreda!"

She dropped the cup she was holding, and in her agitation fell to her knees beside him. He struggled to raise himself, but Elfreda, fearing the shock of seeing her again was too much for him in his weakened state, quickly restrained him and said, "Guy, I must leave thee for now, and thou must go to sleep again."

A faint smile parted the patient's lips. "Art thou sure we are not in old Nathan's house in London," he said, "and thou prescribing thy usual remedy?"

"Nay, we are not in London; but thou must follow my commands even as thou didst there;" and, to make sure that there was no further agitation, Elfreda instantly withdrew. But Guy could not sleep, and as soon as Elfreda had gone he recollected—what he had forgotten in the transport of meeting her once more—that she was one of the heretic Vaudois whom he had hoped and prayed to see rooted out of the earth.

A groan of almost mortal agony at this thought, and the fear that the curse of the old monk of Crowland might repeat itself in Elfreda's ears,

MADONNA: *statues of Mary, the mother of Jesus*
TRANSPORT: *delight*

broke from his lips, and brought his cousin again to his side to inquire as to the cause.

"Ah, 'tis an old wound, Elfreda, but one that no mortal power can heal," groaned the knight.

"Is it the old curse?" whispered Elfreda, "that which hath shadowed all my life, and which prompted my attempt to destroy myself in the hope of removing it from my friends?"

"Didst thou attempt self-destruction?" hurriedly asked Guy.

Elfreda bowed. "When I left thee and old Nathan it was to drown myself in the sea we had just crossed," she said. "But God in His mercy rescued me, and now He hath shown me that the curse I could not bear hath already been borne by another, and completely removed."

"Our family curse—the curse of the Ericsons— gone! lifted by the Church, and I never knew it!" gasped Guy.

"Nay, the Church hath no power to take away the curse of sin—the Lord Jesus Christ only can do that," answered Elfreda boldly, yet trembling with anxiety.

Guy looked into her earnest face. "Go on," he said; "tell me how thou didst learn that this dreadful curse hath been lifted from our family."

"Nay, I may not tell thee all the story of my life since I left thee, for thou art weak and feeble; yet I will tell it to thee some day, and then thou wilt learn more fully of my meaning; but now I will give thee a few words to think of that have been of great comfort to me: 'For Christ also hath once suffered for sins, the just for the unjust, that he might bring us to God.'"[1] Guy looked up as if for some explanation of these words, and seeing this, Elfreda went on:

"Dost thou not see that if Christ hath suffered once for the sins of men, it were an insult to say that we, too, will bear their sins—as though His suffering or holiness were not sufficient without us? If that old monk sinned we cannot, and God doth not call us to, bear the punishment of his sin, for Christ hath already borne it for him and for us also, and so there can be no curse."

"But the Church, Elfreda—the Church saith the curse is not removed."

Elfreda hardly knew how to meet this question now without deeply agitating her cousin, for she knew his strong devotion to the Church, and how could she rudely tell him, what had cost her weeks of agony in the discovery, that the Church was wrong in many things which she taught—false to the high trust committed to her care. So she said gently:

"Guy, dost thou know upon what the Church foundeth her teaching and practice?"

"Yes, upon the teaching of the holy apostles," replied Guy.

"That which is contained in the Word of God, which we call the Scriptures," said Elfreda.

[1] I PETER 3:18

"Yes, the Scriptures, and the teaching of saints who lived after the apostles," replied Guy.

"But since they lived in later times, and had themselves to learn from the writings of the apostles, it were better for us also to go back to these writings, and learn what God Himself would say to us by His first witnesses."

"It were better, perhaps," assented Guy; "but since the Church hath decreed that the holy Scriptures should not be read by the unlearned—"

"But why should she so order if all her teaching hath the warranty of God's Word? That I may not weary thee with talking, however," she added, "I will ask thee to read this Scripture of the Gospel history for thyself; and then we will some other time talk further upon this matter."

Saying this Elfreda darted away, and before Guy could refuse or expostulate, a beautiful manuscript of the Gospels was placed in his hands by his beloved cousin.

EXPOSTULATE: *protest*

Chapter XIX

The Wounded Knight

GUY had no intention of reading the manuscript Elfreda brought him, for he knew the
Scriptures had been forbidden by the Church, and
he stood in too much awe of her power to break
her laws lightly. Besides, he had a grave suspicion
that reading the Scriptures savored of that heresy
which he had vowed and endeavored to root out of
Languedoc, and so for awhile the parchment roll
was laid aside. But as he grew stronger the desire
for something to break the dreary monotony of his
lonely hours overcame his scruples, and Elfreda,
who had purposely kept away from him as much as
possible, saw at last, to her great joy, that her cousin
had begun the perusal of her precious book. She
avoided making any allusion to this, however, and
Guy carefully concealed it whenever De Montfort
or any of his friends visited him.

The weeks slipped on, and news came that
Count Raymond had gone in person to Rome,
hoping to move the pope's clemency, and induce

SCRUPLES: *restraints*
PERUSAL: *reading*

him to command the withdrawal of De Montfort's host. How the unfortunate count fared in his mission Elfreda could not hear; she only knew that the peaceful, helpless Vaudois, whose sole crime was that they dared to profess a purer faith than the Church taught, were driven from their homes, and hunted from town to town, on to the very fastnesses of the Alps and Apennines, and that on every road their bones lay bleaching.

All this Elfreda heard; and Guy heard it, too, but it failed to awaken any thrill of triumph in his heart now, for he also was beginning to learn by slow degrees—yet nonetheless surely—that the Church was not the pure fountain of wisdom, truth, and love he had hitherto believed her to be.

He determined to question Elfreda as to the mode of life and worship practiced by these "poor men," Vaudois, or Albigenses, as they were variously called. If she were one of them she had surely been admitted to all their secret rites of worship, he reasoned, however horrible they might be, and she would know the secret of their lives, too, whether they did practice such gross immorality as was laid to their charge.

The fact that Elfreda had embraced their faith made him doubt some of the tales he had heard concerning them, for surely one so gentle and pure-minded as his cousin would shrink with horror from the vile orgies such as he believed they indulged in. It was with no great surprise, therefore,

ORGIES: *wild rituals*

that he listened to her account of the holy, blameless lives led by these people, or that the horrible part of their worship consisted only in their rejection of all images, pictures, or signs—of even the cross—and that prayer, reading the Scriptures, and expounding them, formed the chief part of their worship. Elfreda sometimes felt anxious to learn what was passing in her cousin's mind, but it was some time before he spoke. At length he startled her with the question: "Elfreda, hast thou ever heard whether God will forgive unconfessed sin?"

Elfreda looked puzzled at the question. "Nay, but it is our bounden duty to confess our sins to God, though I hold it not needful to confess to a priest," she said.

"But hast thou never felt, when thou didst go to confession, that thy memory would not recall all those things that ought to be confessed; and, after the confessor had given his absolution and benediction, and, perhaps, as thou wert rising from thy knees, or going from his presence, some great lapse of duty that ought to have been confessed hath suddenly recurred to thy mind, and thou hast gone away burdened in conscience, and feeling that the word of blessing were but a mockery?"

"It hath sometimes troubled me, as thou sayest, but not of late; for I can go to God at any time and confess my sins without fear of wearying Him. Besides, Christ died to pardon all my sins, those which I forget as well as those which I confess. It is not confession, but Christ that taketh away our sins, and knowing this, how can I be afraid if I believe in Him?"

"This faith of thine would certainly be good for warriors such as I—for men who, while they fear that each confession may be their last, are at the same time tortured with the thought that they have forgotten some sin which should have been remembered: some sin, perhaps, so great that the pardon of all else will avail nothing while it remains unforgiven. O, Elfreda, it is a terrible thing to live in such fear as this!"

"But it is not the will of God that any should live in such fear. He hath called us to freedom and joy, not to bondage and fear. We are His children, dearly and tenderly beloved, and He would have us believe in this love—believing that He so loved us as to give His Son to die for us, 'the just for the unjust, that He might bring us to God.' No saint could do this, or God would not have given up His Son to perform the work; therefore, to seek the help of saints or angels is a vain and foolish thing."

"Thou art in very truth a heretic, my Elfreda," said Guy, smiling faintly; but he did not shudder when he pronounced the word "heretic," as he once did.

"Nay, nay, I am no heretic, Guy. I have but learned to love the Lord Jesus Christ a little in return for His great love to me, and I would that thou, too—"

"Thou wouldst fain have a Knight Hospitaler break his vows and turn heretic, too," interrupted Guy; but there was a touch of grave earnestness in his tone, and Elfreda forebore to make any further remark.

That the Spirit of God was at work in Guy's heart Elfreda fully believed, and so she was content to wait, and watch, and pray, leaving to God the time when her cousin should arrive at a full knowledge of these truths. They could not be received all at once, she knew. There was much to be unlearned first. Many a hard battle must be fought, and many a cherished prejudice given up; and hardest of all, perhaps, every good work as a ground of merit must be laid aside before the simple, humbling message of the Gospel could be accepted in all its fullness. But she could trust that He who had taught her, and led her into this full Gospel liberty, would likewise teach and lead Guy by the help of the Scriptures he was now diligently studying.

The cousins had both fondly hoped that no suspicions had been entertained of Elfreda being other than an orthodox Catholic, but in this they were deceived. The attendant who came daily to the bower to bring her food, and all that was requisite for her patient, had soon noticed the absence of all those objects of adoration so clear to a devout follower of the Church. This absence was not only noticeable in the furniture and arrangements of the apartment, but also in her own

ORTHODOX: *faithful*
REQUISITE: *required*

person. She wore neither cross, reliquary, nor rosary, and surely one who had heard the eloquent Dominic preach ought to avail herself of the last blessed invention. So reasoned her wary attendant; but he did not communicate his suspicions to anyone else, or speak to her upon this matter; he kept up a silent, constant, stealthy watch upon every movement of both nurse and patient. What he saw going on from day to day soon convinced him that Elfreda was a heretic, and he had no doubt this wounded knight held the same detestable doctrines, else why should she be so constant in her attendance upon him.

So as soon as Guy began to improve in health he too was watched, whenever the man had an opportunity. He soon noticed the mysterious parchment roll, hastily put out of sight when he appeared, and noted, too, that the patient never asked for a cross or crucifix to be hung up in his room.

Now if he could only make sure that these two were heretics, and give information against them that would be at once conclusive, it might be of great service in bringing him under the notice of De Montfort or the archbishop of Rouen. Orders had been given by the bishops that anyone suspecting others of holding or teaching doctrines contrary to those commanded by the Church should at once give information against them, and so the attendant was not long in informing some of his superiors of a conversation he had overheard

RELIQUARY: *a small box containing relics*

between this strange nurse and her patient, in which she had said that, "To seek the aid of the saints, as the Church commanded, was a vain and foolish thing," and that the knight had listened to this without reproving her.

At first the man's words were disregarded, for De Valery was too earnest and devout a Catholic to be thought capable of such heresy; but to make sure of this beyond a doubt, another was set to watch, and report all that he heard or saw. He had not to practice his inquisitorial work long before he gained ample proof that De Valery, as well as his nurse, had embraced the detestable heresy of the Vaudois; and the very next day Guy was visited by two of his brother knights, who questioned and cross-questioned him at some length, and finally told him of the accusation that had been brought against him.

He did not deny the truth of the charge. "I am learning many things I had not thought to find in this Word of God given to us in the Scriptures," he said.

"Then thou hast broken thy vows, and instead of fighting against the enemies of the cross and holy Church, in the day of battle, hast deserted the sacred standard, and become a corrupt and unsound member of our holy brotherhood."

And having said this the two knight-monks departed, and Guy hastily called Elfreda to his side and told her what had happened.

INQUISITORIAL: *prying*

"Thou must escape from the castle, if possible, tonight, for I shall doubtless be removed from thy care without delay," said Guy. "Elfreda, we shall never meet again on this side of the grave; but in heaven, where God Himself will be our teacher and guide, all doubts and mysteries will be made clear. I can believe this, my Elfreda, that Christ hath died to redeem me, hath pardoned all my sins, and the rest I shall learn on the other side of death's dark stream. Farewell, dear, dear Elfreda —dearer today than ever before. The Church separates us now, but God will unite us by and by. Make thy way to England as soon as thou canst, and tell my poor sorrow-stricken mother the good news thou hast taught me. And now take my mantle and wrap it about thee as soon as it is dark, and before thou canst be made prisoner, escape by the secret passage thou hast told me of."

But Elfreda shook her head. "I will never leave thee, Guy," she said. "If they take thee to the dungeons under the castle, I may be able to help thee if I am at hand."

"Nay, my Elfreda," said Guy, "thou must grant this, my last request. I shall be tried on this charge of heresy, and never suffered to leave the castle alive; but let me have the comfort of knowing thou art safe."

Elfreda might still have persisted in her refusal, but that at this moment the door was suddenly opened and two guards appeared, who announced that they were to remove the knight at once to another part of the castle.

Elfreda turned pale. "I obey thee now," she said, casting one more anxious look at her cousin's worn face, and the next minute she had quietly removed the long dark cloak, and having secured the door of the bower against all intruders, she waited until the guard had departed with their prisoner. Then, before they could return for her, she had thrown back the secret sliding panel that opened upon a small steep stairway built in the thickness of the wall. Guided by her hands, she groped her way down through the darkness, hoping to be able to find the secret door of egress from the castle. She was almost unconscious of the flight of time, at first, in her eagerness to reach the outer air, but groped on and on, cutting her hands against the rough, rocky sides of the stairways and passages, which seemed to her interminable.

She must have been thus walking, groping, and crawling for several hours before any outlet could be found; and when she at length stumbled against a door that slowly yielded to her effort to open it, and gave her a sight of the outer world, she was startled to find that the shadows of evening had fallen, and she had only the light of the glittering stars to guide her on her way.

The door, which had swung a little back, appeared like an entrance to the half-ruinous hovel that stood near, and no one would have surmised

EGRESS: *exit*
INTERMINABLE: *endless*

that it led to the stately castle Elfreda had recently left. It was a piece of waste ground on which she stood, tangled and overgrown with weeds, while the castle was far away in the distance, and the town too.

Elfreda had only time to notice these things when she heard a footstep approaching, and she at once concealed herself behind some of the overgrown bushes. Presently another footstep was heard, and then another; until Elfreda, peeping from her hiding-place, saw about a dozen men and women gathered around the first comer.

"Now, my friends," said a quiet, manly voice, "we will have a few verses from the Word of life." And then, slowly and distinctly, Elfreda heard the words of Paul in his Epistle to the Ephesians given to this poor hunted band of Christians—their only comfort and solace now.

There was no light, and at first Elfreda was puzzled to know how the pastor read in the darkness; but she soon discovered, from some words that fell from the bystanders' lips, that these words of the Scriptures were being repeated from memory— that the man had learned them by heart.

Elfreda would not disturb the little meeting until they had concluded their devotions; but she had no fear now, for she felt herself among friends, and when they rose from their knees, and the pastor was bidding each good night, Elfreda stepped softly from her hiding place, startling the little company by her sudden and strange appearance. Her face and hands were cut and bleeding, and her clothes hung in rags about her. Several feared she was a spy, set to watch them, in accordance with the new inquisitorial order of the pope and bishops, but Elfreda soon reassured them.

"I, too, am in peril for the faith of Christ, my Savior," she said, and then, as one or two ventured near, she told the pastor of her flight from the castle of Beziers, and her anxiety concerning her cousin's fate. They could only shake their heads when she spoke of De Montfort's mercy, for they knew what that meant; but one of the women volunteered to take her to her home, and attend to her immediate wants, and this offer Elfreda gladly accepted.

Chapter XX

Outlawed by the Church

ELFREDA could not be persuaded to leave Beziers. Day after day and week after week she hovered about the castle, reckless of her own danger, in hope of hearing from some passing soldier something that might throw light upon her cousin's fate. But the darkness of the grave seemed to have closed round Guy; and at last, as the short winter began again to give way to the genial spring, hope died out of Elfreda's heart, and she resolved to wait only until the season was sufficiently advanced to allow of traveling with less discomfort before setting out for England.

One day as she lingered near the castle, gazing at its lofty towers, and thinking of all that she had seen and heard within its walls, she was startled by seeing a worn, bent figure approaching. Her sympathies were at once enlisted. Some poor pastor had crept back to the scene of his former labors, she thought, while she watched his feeble, tottering footsteps; but something in his manner as he

GENIAL: *pleasant*

drew nearer caused her heart to beat quicker. It must be—yes, it was—her cousin Guy, and she rushed forward to meet him.

With a warning gesture Guy gently repulsed her, fearing that they might yet be within sight of the castle gates. So Elfreda, with a quickened step and heightened color, passed on. She had learned all the turns and windings of the tortuous streets by this time, and so, turning in an apparently opposite direction to that taken by Guy, she yet contrived to meet him before he had gone far along the road.

"This is, indeed, an unspeakable mercy," said Guy as Elfreda once more joined him. "They have turned me out, as a disgraced and degraded knight, to die like a dog in the streets of this strange town; but God hath once more sent his angel to deliver me from death;" and as he spoke he took Elfreda's hand and clasped it in his. "Mine, mine at last, Elfreda," he whispered; "the Church hath set me free from my vows and cast me out as an accursed man, but—"

"Nay, nay, say no more at this time," said Elfreda. "I must take thee to the Jew who so kindly befriended me after old Nathan's death; he hath in charge certain jewels and costly cups of mine and in exchange for these he will willingly give us shelter, and all we may need to take us back to England."

Guy was in no fit condition to travel at present;

REPULSED HER: *kept her back*
TORTUOUS: *twisting*

but the Jew, seeing a chance of driving a good bargain, readily agreed to shelter them, and supply all that was possible to restore his enfeebled health.

When Guy was comfortably settled at the Jew's house, Elfreda went, at his request, to summon the pastor of the Vaudois Church, who still lingered in the neighborhood ministering to the wants of a few of his scattered flock. She knew her cousin desired to join the persecuted Church, although he intended to return to England so soon, but she was surprised at the haste and eagerness he now manifested to have this done at once.

Great caution had to be exercised in bringing the pastor to the Jew's residence, not only on their own account, but on that of their host also; for now there were many who spent their whole time in watching to detect heresy and heretics. But the good man came after nightfall without any to interrupt him, and, after a long conversation with Guy, Elfreda was sent for to take part in the conference. She was hardly prepared for the eager question Guy put to her as she entered.

"Wilt thou be my wife? wilt thou suffer this holy minister of God's truth to join our hands tonight, even as our hearts have long been united?"

Elfreda looked from her cousin to the pastor. "But—but—we are of kin," she faltered.

"I have hidden nothing concerning our kinship, Elfreda, and this good man saith he knoweth nothing in God's law to forbid our wedding. If we were powerful nobles the pope would readily grant us a dispensation to marry—provided always that we could pay him a sufficient bribe, although the Church doth forbid it."

"I have little care for the voice of the Church," said Elfreda, "but thy vows, Guy, and thy friends in England—"

"As for my vows," interrupted Guy; "the Church hath annulled them, and, being taken in ignorance, I gladly ratify the sentence of degradation lately passed upon me; and as for my friends, thou knowest I have had no friend like thyself since thou gavest me as my watchword and battle cry, 'Christ and His salvation.' I have been a long time learning the meaning of those words, Elfreda, but Christ hath set me free at last—free from the guilt and bondage of my own sin, and free, too, from the bondage the Church in her tyranny would impose upon us."

Elfreda yielded, at last, to the earnest pleadings of her cousin, and there, in the presence of the Jew's family, she was married by the old pastor of the Vaudois Church. Her host would fain have had some little feasting and rejoicing on this occasion, but Elfreda begged that the marriage might be kept as secret as possible. Guy's health, too, had to be considered; but now that she was able to devote herself unremittingly to her care of him he gained strength quite rapidly.

It was a peaceful, happy month that these storm-

DISPENSATION: *exemption from the law of the Church*
ANNULLED: *canceled*
RATIFY: *confirm*

tossed hearts passed beneath the old Jew's roof at Beziers, and it was almost with a feeling of reluctance that they bade *adieu* to their kind host, and set out on their journey toward the north.

They could travel with less fear now, for Guy had wonderfully improved in health and spirits, and the jewels Elfreda had sold enabled them to maintain the appearance of wealthy people. None would be likely to recognize Guy in his merchant's dress as the disgraced and enfeebled Knight Hospitaler, who had been turned out of the castle to die in the streets. Elfreda, too, seemed suddenly to have grown young again; but she gladly turned her back upon the country where God's saints were so cruelly persecuted, hoping that in England they might be permitted to worship Him in peace.

They often beguiled the hours of travel by talking of their distant but beloved native land. Not so fair or sunny as bright Languedoc, she could yet boast of green fields and mighty forests unblighted by such a terrible crusade as that now waging against these southern provinces of France; and though her people were less polite and polished, there was a stern truthfulness and uprightness in them which these light-hearted people could not even comprehend. Pleasure seemed the whole end and aim of life to the one; duty was the watchword of the other.

Hours and days thus flew by, until at last they came once more within sight of the white cliffs of

WATCHWORD: *motto*
ADIEU: *farewell*
BEGUILED: *passed*

Dover. Scarcely, however, had they set foot on shore before they were met with the news that King John had offended the pope by refusing to receive Archbishop Langton, whom he had appointed to the see of Canterbury, and for this offense the whole kingdom was laid under an interdict. Though the sun was shining brightly a dreadful gloom seemed to be brooding over everything—a silent, nameless something that seemed to strike a chill to the heart, bowed every head, and checked every joy.

No church bell rang now for *matins* or *vespers*, for the churches were all closed. Sundays and holy days were like all the rest, and often as they passed along the roads they would come upon a dead body thrown into a ditch without any funeral rites, for none dare speak when the Church commanded silence.

Sometimes a priest, more merciful than his brethren, would stealthily baptize an infant in the church porch, or marry a couple who had waited month after month in the vain hope that the interdict would be mercifully removed by the holy father at Rome. But there seemed little prospect of this at present, for King John had seized the Church lands, and was using them for his own purposes; while most of the bishops had fled from the country to take refuge in France or Rome.

It was with a feeling of heart-sickness and sorrow that Guy and his wife at length reached London, where it was arranged that Elfreda should stay

SEE: *seat of authority*

for a short time; while Guy went to Bourne in the disguise of a cheapman, to learn, if possible, whether any news of himself had reached his friends of late. There was a double need for caution, for if it was discovered that the degraded Knight Hospitaler still lived, he might be seized by one of the preceptories that were established in England, and tried again for his heresy, and for breaking his vows by marrying; and if it were known whom he had married, the Church would excommunicate them both. It was, of course, their great desire to live as quietly as possible, so as not to excite any attention among their neighbors or friends as to their remissness in observing the duties imposed by the Church. Whether this could be safely attempted in the neighborhood of Guy's old home was a problem he was anxious to solve as soon as he could.

Elfreda had brought with her the legal documents left by old Nathan, establishing her right to her property, the bulk of which he had, with prudent forethought, transferred to some of his brethren in London. They labored, therefore, under no inconvenience from want of means. Elfreda was possessed of wealth sufficient for the wants of both as long as they lived. Still, it was thought more prudent that he should go to Bourne with a pack of merchandise on his shoulders; for it would be easy to gain admission to the castle as a cheapman, and it would give him an excuse to ask for all the family under the plea of selling his wares.

REMISSNESS: *carelessness*
WANT OF MEANS: *lack of money*

It was the third day after leaving London that Guy, with his pack on his shoulder, sat down to rest in a thick hazel copse which he knew was on the borders of a wood reported to be infested by the most daring band of outlaws in England. But he had little fear of them now, for he was not the wealthy knight of Bourne, but the humble pack-man of London, and these outlaws would rather give to the poor than rob them. So when a sudden shout which he knew to be the outlaws' cry—"St. George for merrie England"—came, borne upon the summer breeze, and quickly followed by the sound of crackling boughs and hasty footsteps, Guy did not move, but calmly waited for the coming of the robbers.

He had not to wait long. Two or three broke through the bushes, and stood before him the next minute.

"Ho, sir cheapman! whither away?" asked one, eyeing Guy curiously.

"Canst thou tell me whether the Castle of Bourne be in this neighborhood?" asked Guy, preparing to unfasten his pack, that the robbers might see its contents, and thus be assured that he trusted them. In this way, he thought, he might learn what changes had taken place in his old home during his absence.

These men, shut out from the world, were as eager to look at the knives and drinking horns, gilt bodkins, and pieces of embroidered silk, as children to look at toys; and while they were examining the different articles, passing them from hand to hand, Guy was questioning one and another upon the business of the neighborhood and the inhabitants of the castle, which he knew lay just beyond these woods.

"The late baron, Sir Valence de Valery, was a true knight to Saxon and Norman alike; but Sir Gilbert, who now reigns as lord of Bourne, is more occupied with public matters, though he favors not King John in his oppressive rule."

"Then Sir Valence is dead. When did he die?" asked the cheapman, with great difficulty restraining his emotion.

"Nay, I cannot tell thee that, but 'tis two or three summers I know," replied the outlaw, turning over the contents of the pack at his pleasure.

"And the lady, his wife—doth she still live at the castle?" asked Guy.

"Yes; Sir Gilbert is not married, and so his mother still rules among her bower-maidens there, although she hath seldom been seen beyond the castle garden since news came of the death of Sir Guy, her oldest and best beloved son."

"Where did he die?" asked Guy.

"Nay, sir packman, thou canst know but little of the men of the merry greenwood if thou dost count them able to remember the names of all the places travelers tell of. We can bend a bow, and strike the mark at a greater distance than any other men in England, but we know little of travelers' arts beyond filling our pouches with their gold. 'Twas beyond seas, of course, and I have heard it whispered that the young knight was outlawed by holy Church for some offense, which I deem was unwise, since the Church hath all the power in this world, and the next too, or our blessed image of Saint Mary would not now be lying on the ground, and all merry-making at an end, as it is today in England."

"It is, I trow, a sorry time for our merrie England while groaning under this interdict; but King John will surely receive this archbishop of the pope's choosing ere long."

"He will if aught can be gained by it," said the outlaw contemptuously, "and if not, he will hold to his obstinacy until the pope or the barons compel him to submit."

"The barons!" exclaimed Guy as he began to collect his wares together, "do they think of the wild scheme of restoring Saxon rule?"

"Nay; either Saxon or Norman can rob us of our liberty, and it will be to secure this—to place it beyond the power of such tyrants as John—that the barons will rise."

To Guy, who had been away from England for several years, and knew little of the progress of public events, the man's words seemed as an idle tale. The king and the barons had always united in oppressing the people, and for their interests ever to be divided seemed incredible. He was careful, however, not to let the outlaw see that he doubted the correctness of his information or conclusions, and, giving the leader of the party a knife which he seemed to admire, he shouldered his pack once more, and took his way through the wood toward his brother's castle.

Chapter XXI

At Bourne Once More

THE visit of a cheapman to the Castle of Bourne was not an event of frequent occurrence; and in those days of doublets, and gaily plumed hats, and bedizened cloaks, and other masculine finery, the men servants and retainers, as well as the maids and their mistress, would hail the coming of the traveling merchant. So the portcullis was raised and the drawbridge lowered almost as soon as Guy had blown the old horn hanging at the gate, and once more he stood in the great hall of his old home.

It was not easy to play the part of a humble packman as he recognized one and another of the old retainers, some of whom had carried him in their arms when a boy, and had given him his first lessons in hawking or bending the bow, and holding the lance. But for Elfreda's sake, as well as his own, he must meet the inquiring gaze of each as they asked him the news of the day, for to be a successful merchant, he must be a social gossip

BEDIZENED: *showy*
PORTCULLIS: *a strong iron grating*

and traveling newsman as well. So, while the contents of the pack were being spread out on the long oaken table, he answered the questions of one and another as well as he could, detailing the scraps of news he had been able to collect along the road concerning the progress of the war now being waged against the Welsh, who had once more revolted from English rule.

It was easy to see that King John was hated here as cordially as his brother Richard had been loved, and the reason was easily discovered. The weak, treacherous monarch lived in continual dread that his life would be taken by some of his alienated subjects, and so, to secure himself against any such treachery on the part of his barons, he had compelled them each to send a son or daughter as hostage to one of the king's royal castles, where they served as pages or bower-maidens to Queen Isabella; and Sir Gilbert's youngest brother, the pet and darling of the household, had just been dragged from them by the king's order to attend the queen, who was now imprisoned in Gloucester Abbey.

"'Tis a sorrowful household thou hast happened upon," said one of the maids, as she looked at a bright-colored kerchief Guy had just put down. "First came the death of our late lord, whereat our lady well-nigh broke her heart, for he who should have stood in his father's place was beyond the seas, and a Knight Hospitaler to boot; so there was naught for it but that the young Sir Gilbert should rule in his stead.

"And the lady—doth she grieve still that her son became a Knight Hospitaler?" asked Guy as the girl suddenly stopped her recital, captivated by the beauty of a sharp-pointed silver bodkin.

"Nay, sorer grief hath fallen upon her since, for news came from beyond seas that he had disgraced the holy order and had died."

"And she mourneth his death or his disgrace?" asked Guy a little anxiously.

One of the women looked up in his face with an arch smile, and said, "'Tis easy to see thou art not a father or thou wouldst not ask such a question. Our lady holdeth that he was unlawfully degraded, and sorely mourneth for his loss. She hath not held up her head since the tidings came, and now that her youngest son is taken to be page to the imprisoned queen, she is as one crushed with the weight of her sorrow. And our lord, Sir Gilbert, talketh wildly sometimes of the barons rising to defend the liberties of the people from the tyranny they suffer."

But Guy had only half-understood the latter part of her speech; he could think only of his mother shut up in her bower, lonely, desolate, with a burden of anguish crushing her, and no comforter, no Savior such as the Scriptures revealed, to console her in her great affliction. He almost hated the friendly pack which had secured his entrance to the castle when he saw the articles passed round

ARCH: *playful*

from hand to hand, their qualities and prices discussed, and thought of his mother upstairs pining
in her lonely desolation, and he unable to give her
one word of comfort.

At length he resolved to see her at least. He had
provided himself with a few jewels, which he carried in a small case concealed beneath his doublet,
and he now begged one of the maids to inform
her mistress of his arrival, and to ask her to inspect
his wares, as he had a few gems to sell that he had
just brought from beyond the seas.

At the mention of their mistress' coming everyone laid down their selected bargain, that she
might have the first choice of the wares, for the
girl had said, "If thou dost come from beyond the
seas my mistress will doubtless see thee;" and she
had gone at once to tell her lady, while the falconer and his assistants went to attend to the feeding
of the hawks and birds under their care, and the
various household servants resumed their labors,
leaving the great hall in the possession of the pack-
man and a few old retainers.

Guy busied himself in rearranging his wares to
hide his emotion, for the thought of so soon seeing his widowed mother well-nigh overcame all his
firmness.

It was some little time, however, before the stately Lady de Valery entered the great hall, and it was
with evident indifference that she came forward
and looked at the things displayed on the table.
Guy, of course, stood at a humble distance while

the lady of the castle made her inspection, and was thankful that he was not required to speak, but could gaze at his mother in silence for a few minutes. She was greatly changed. The fair, proud face was deeply lined with care and sorrow, and the golden hair was almost white now. Guy could with difficulty restrain himself from throwing his arms around her when she motioned him to come nearer.

Of course, as a money-making merchant he ought to have recommended his goods, and praised their peculiar merits and cheapness. But poor Guy was quite unequal to this task now. He could only name the price of the articles the lady selected, and this he did in a sort of hoarse whisper, which made the attendant bower-maidens wonder what had suddenly ailed the cheapman.

As Lady de Valery, however, was turning away Guy made a mighty effort to check back his rising sobs, and said, "Nay, my lady, thou hast not seen all my store."

Lady de Valery started, and turned back instantly as he spoke. She looked scarcely less confused than the cheapman now, and the little crowd of retainers and bower-maidens standing at a distance could only stare in open-eyed wonder at the strange scene.

"I have some gems I would fain show the Lady de Valery—gems which I brought from across the sea," continued Guy.

"Thou hast but lately come from beyond the seas?" said the lady, questioningly.

"I have, but tarried a few days in London ere I set out for Lincoln and Northampton, whose worthy Archdeacon Grosseteste hath some knowledge of me." Guy scarcely knew what he said, but as he drew the jewel-case from his doublet he leaned forward and said in a whisper, "This Archdeacon Grosseteste knew thy son, Sir Guy de Valery, when he was in Paris."

The lady started, and turned pale; but she understood that the man had some news to impart concerning her son, and bidding him put up the jewels again, she said, "I am weary now, but tarry awhile and refresh thyself, and I will see these jewels anon," and she turned away, followed by her maids.

Guy was not kept waiting long, for the lady was as anxious as he was for this interview; and he had scarcely concluded the meal that had been placed ready for him by his mother's command before one of the maids again appeared, saying her mistress would see him and examine the jewels in the bower.

How Guy's heart beat as he once more ascended the narrow stone stairs and approached the door of his mother's room!

The lady had sent some of her maids away, only two of her oldest attendants being present, and they were silently employed with their distaffs in a recess at some distance from where their mistress sat.

Guy took out the jewel-case, and humbly presented the gems on bended knees for the lady's inspection. But she scarcely glanced at them.

"Thou didst see my son—my Guy—before he died?" she said with breathless eagerness.

Guy bowed his head.

"Did—did he think of his mother—charge thee with any message for me?" she asked.

"He was most desirous to send thee word concerning a certain curse," answered Guy, hardly knowing what to say.

"My poor Guy! he, too, hath fallen a victim to the curse of the Ericsons," said the lady in a tone of bitter anguish.

"Nay, nay, my lady! but Guy knoweth now that there is no curse—no curse but sin, and that hath been borne by the great Sin-bearer, Jesus Christ. Mother, Mother, dost thou not know me?" and Guy, completely overcome, buried his face in her lap, as he used to do when a child.

But the lady neither spoke nor moved, and when Guy looked up again he feared that the sudden shock had killed her. The maids hurried forward as he cried for help, and various restoratives were applied—feathers burned under her nostrils, and shavings of hartshorn when the milder remedy failed. But with all the chafings and bathings and burnings, it was nearly an hour before Lady de Valery again opened her eyes, and her first words

RECESS: *alcove*

made her attendants fear that her mind was affect-
ed. "Guy! Guy! where is my son, Guy?" she asked
feebly; and Guy, who had thought it prudent for
her sake to retire to a distant corner of the room,
came forward, to the evident disgust of the maids,
who would have sent him away if they dared. Again
he kneeled down, and took the thin white hand
in his, kissing it tenderly, as he had often done in
the old days when he talked hopefully of being a
knight, and winning his mother's favor at the tournament.

The well-remembered caress proved a far more
powerful restorative than any that had been applied yet, and the lady seemed to throw off the remains of her lethargy at once.

"Guy, Guy, let me hold thee in my arms, my son!"
she said, eagerly bending over him. "They told me
thou wert dead, and worse than dead—disgraced,"
she whispered.

Guy trembled as his mother folded her arms
about him, and for a moment he almost regretted that he had undeceived her, for it would be a
cruel blow to her when she heard that he was an
outlaw—worse, far worse than a robber of the forest—an outlaw of the Church.

But it had to be told after some little time, for
Lady de Valery, having recovered her consciousness, questioned him so closely that he was obliged
to confess at last that he had been degraded from
his position as a Knight Hospitaler because he had
avowed his belief that Christ alone had redeemed

LETHARGY: *drowsiness*

him and all men without the help of saints or angels, and that He, of His own pure love and goodwill, would save all who come to Him, without the
intercession of the Virgin mother or any created
being.

"But, my son, the Church teacheth us that it
is needful to seek the aid of saints," said Lady de
Valery.

"I know it, my mother; but I know, too, that in
this, as well as in many other matters, she hath
departed from the pure teachings of the Gospel
which she first held. Errors have crept in again and
again, and instead of casting out these stumbling-
blocks, which defiled the fountain of living waters,
the Church hath piled them up one upon another,
well-nigh choking the spring, and hiding it from
men's eyes while they perish with thirst. When our
Church hath purged herself from the cruelty and
treachery which she doeth continually, and casts
down this grim wall of errors and superstitions
which she hath slowly built up between God and
man, then will Guy de Valery once more bow to
her teaching and her authority, but until then he
will cleave to Christ alone, and be the outlaw of
the Church."

"Nay, but, my son, thou canst not judge the
Church; thou hast but little learning save in the
use of sword and battle-ax. Listen to me, Guy; I
have long wished, and now am determined, to
retire from this, my home, and spend the last of

my days in penitence and retirement at Crowland. Do thou follow me thither, and seek by prayer and fasting to be united to holy Church once more."

"Nay, mother, it were useless to ask me. I have more learning than thou dost think, for I retired to a monastery before I became a Knight Hospitaler, and spent many hours among the books in the monastery library, and—and I can never again take monkish vows now that the Church hath annulled those already taken, for I have married a wife since—one who believes with me in Christ and His salvation."

Lady de Valery did not ask who this was, for her mind instantly reverted to Gilbert, and she wondered how he would receive his brother now that he had come home to claim his inheritance. But Guy quickly relieved her fears upon this point.

"My mother, thou knowest that I am thy son Guy; but to the world I am dead, and must remain so. I cannot even bear my lawful name of De Valery, but have taken thine, my mother, and must be known as the humble cheapman, Ericson, if I would live in peace."

Lady de Valery groaned. It was a cruel blow to her pride, as well as her love, that her eldest—her darling, should be compelled to shelter himself under the despised, hated Saxon name; but her love conquered at last, and to see him alive, and in the full strength of manhood, was joy enough to compensate for all besides, and as she looked into his calm, peaceful face, she thought God could not have cast off her son though the Church had, or he would not wear so serene a brow.

The whisper had already gone forth in the castle that the humble cheapman was no other than Sir Guy de Valery, but the lady did not deem it wise to confirm this at once. She would wait until Gilbert returned from his journey to the north, and meanwhile Guy could stay there as her guest. But this he was unwilling to do, for several reasons. It would confirm the suspicions already aroused, and they would speedily have a visit from Crowland Minster that might prove unpleasant in its consequences.

So, after spending one night at his old ancestral home, Guy shouldered his pack once more and went on to Lincoln, and thence to Northampton, for he had heard that his friend Grosseteste, who was studying at the University of Paris while he was staying there, and with whom he had formed an intimate friendship, had lately been appointed archdeacon, and he was anxious to see him and discover, if possible, where he and Elfreda could fix their home with the least fear of discovery. He wished to settle this point before returning to London or paying another visit to Bourne, for he was anxious to remove Elfreda to a place of safety, and also to assure his brother that he had no intention of claiming his inheritance.

Chapter XXII

Conclusion

IT was sad to pass along the road and see the crosses thrown down, and the sacred images lying with their faces to the ground. It was a terrible evidence of the ruthless power of that Church, as well as of its injustice, that it could thus terrify the superstitious fears of an entire nation, and lay a heavy burden of guilt upon their consciences, while the only offender, because of his lofty position, was allowed to go unpunished, and carry out his tyrannous and iniquitous plans. King John cared little for the interdict that the pope had laid on his land since it did not affect him; but now far-seeing men began to ask each other in cautious whispers whether there was no remedy for their nation's troubles. Since the sight of his people's sufferings did not move King John to comply with the demand of the pope, and since the pope seemed to care nothing for the rights of Englishmen so long as his own power was maintained, would it not be well to try some other mode of securing and preserving their liberties?

INIQUITOUS: *wicked*

Wherever Guy went there was the same anxious stir in men's minds. The interdict, which had at first fallen upon them as a crushing calamity, was growing less irksome as things went on, but the incessant outbreaks of cruelty and treachery on the part of their despicable monarch kept the nation alive to their need of some bulwark for their liberties. Everywhere the eyes of the masses were turned toward the great barons, many of whom ruled as petty kings over their respective districts; for their rights were as often invaded, and their families disgraced, as those of the most insignificant henchmen.

At Lincoln and at Northampton, as well as at all the towns that lay along the route, there were the same whispers, and Guy feared that unless the king changed his policy England would soon be distracted by a great civil war.

At Northampton he found his friend Grosseteste. This famous priest and scholar had recently come from Paris, but because of the interdict could not as yet be inducted into his office as archdeacon. With him Guy spent several welcome hours. And now a hope dawned in his heart that England might yet possess the blessing for which the Vaudois Church now suffered so bitterly, for the archdeacon was as full of plans for reforming the Church as ever Guy could be. Contrary to all his clerical brethren, he advocated the study of the Scriptures, and had himself commenced a

INCESSANT: *constant*
BULWARK: *defense*
HENCHMEN: *squire or page*

translation of the Psalms into the language of the people. This was really a needful undertaking, for the old Saxon version by King Alfred was fast becoming obsolete because of the many changes in the language. He would put down the Feast of Fools at Epiphany, and the drinking of scot ales in the churches wherever he could, and so Guy left Northampton with the full determination to return again shortly, and, if Elfreda liked the place, they would settle there; for under the protection of the liberal-minded Grosseteste there would be less fear of persecution on account of their peculiar opinions.

To Elfreda all places were alike, so long as Guy was not far from her side, and so they soon moved to Northampton, and when comfortably settled Guy went to pay another visit to Bourne. Gilbert was anxiously expecting him, and finding him fully determined not to claim his inheritance, he insisted upon his receiving a tithe for all the lands of Bourne.

"I shall never marry," said Gilbert; "I mean to devote myself to the freeing this our merrie England from the power of such tyrants as King John."

"How dost thou purpose doing this?" asked Guy, a little anxiously.

Gilbert shook his head. "Adelais' husband, as well as several other barons, would proclaim a war; thou didst hear that our sister married our old foe, De Grantham?"

LIBERAL-MINDED: *open-minded*
TITHE: *tenth part of the yearly income*
PURPOSE: *propose*

"It were well to end all feuds thus," said Guy with a smile; "but what sayest thou to De Grantham's proposal?" he asked.

"That the time is not ripe for it. These people of England are moved but slowly even to redress their wrongs, and I would advocate peaceable measures. Didst thou ever meet with this archbishop, who dare not set foot in the realm, whom the pope hath appointed and the king will not accept? He is an Englishman, it is said."

"Yes, Stephen Langton is an Englishman—was a fellow-student with Pope Innocent, but will not prove his easy tool. I have seen one who knows him well, and who says Langton's sympathies are neither with the pope nor the king in this quarrel, but he pities the poor oppressed people who suffer under this interdict."

Gilbert looked at his brother in amazement. "What shall we hear next!" he exclaimed; "this archbishop joining the barons would be scarcely less than wonderful. But now about our lady mother. Since thy visit she seems more than ever determined to retire to a convent, talking about her pride being the curse of the family, and her resolution to conquer it by a life of poverty. What sayest thou?"

"I would that she could be persuaded to stay here and govern thy household until thou dost bring home a wife," said Guy.

But this Lady de Valery could by no means be persuaded to do. She needed humbling for her sins, and so she would retire to a convent, to spend the remainder of her life in fasting and penitence. After some little time, however, she consented to change her original purpose so far that she would go for a year only at first, and that the Abbey of Northampton should be her place of retirement instead of Crowland; for Guy thought if he could be near his mother to converse with her frequently he might be able to lead her to the feet of the Savior, instead of having the pain of knowing she was bowing to a host of vain mediators.

So when her household was set in order Lady de Valery retired to Northampton, where she met Elfreda, but only half-forgave her for persuading Guy to break his allegiance to the Church. She comforted herself, however, with the thought, that if she passed the remainder of her days in penance and prayer the superabundant merit of these good works would surely suffice to win Guy's salvation at last; while Guy was equally sure that in his frequent visits to his mother, and the enlightened teaching of Grosseteste, who was to be her confessor, she would soon learn to abandon these vain services and put her trust in Christ alone.

So the year of probation which Lady de Valery had agreed upon passed away, and nothing beyond the gradual enlightenment of the lady's mind happened to disturb or elate Guy, who lived in the strictest retirement, carefully avoiding all interference with public matters.

Not so Gilbert. He was foremost among the

barons who openly expressed their dissatisfaction with the king's policy, and when the pope, finding that the interdict laid upon the kingdom had no effect upon the rebellious monarch, and the excommunication published in Rome could not be served upon John in person, and therefore was null and void, adopted another and more effectual plan for bringing him to submission. He absolved John's vassals from their oaths of fealty, and called upon all Christian princes and barons to assist in dethroning him.

The favorable opportunity had come at last, thought some, when they heard the startling news, and once more men began to look for the barons to take action at once; but Guy gravely shook his head and set off to Bourne without delay, for he was anxious to see his brother before he took council with the neighboring barons.

He was only just in time, for Gilbert was already preparing to set out on a journey to confer upon the advisability of striking a blow for freedom, and his men-at-arms were busily polishing armor and sharpening battle-axes when Guy appeared.

"Thou wilt join us in this, Guy?" said his brother eagerly when they were left alone together.

But Guy shook his head. "Nay, nay," he said. "I would not help to enslave my country—I would that I could set her free."

"And is it not for freedom we would combine against our cruel tyrant?" asked Gilbert hotly.

VASSALS: *subjects*
ENCROACHMENTS: *advancements*
SUBVERTING: *destroying*

"To free yourselves in this way will be to sell yourselves bondsmen to Rome," replied Guy. "If thou and the rest of England's barons obey this mandate of the pope, who can tell what the next may be? and if the barons can revolt at the will of the pope, kings can trample on their people likewise."

It was not easy at first to convince Gilbert of the fact that the gradual encroachments of the allpowerful Church were subverting the liberty of each individual soul, as well as drawing supreme power to the pontiff, and making him in very truth what he claimed to be, "king of kings and lord of lords." He had not seen the exhibition of cruel persecution that Guy had; but when he heard the story of Count Raymond's wrongs, he at once gave up the project he had formed, and promised to endeavor to persuade his friends to do the same, and wait and watch the course of public events.

They did not have to wait long before there was a call for action. King Philip of France, who had succeeded in wresting all John's continental possessions from him, was only too ready to obey Pope Innocent. What mattered it to him that the price of these conquests was the freedom of his national Church, which had bravely struggled against the innovations of Rome. Fair, fertile Languedoc was owned by one of his barons now, and was in vassalage to him; and if England could be made an appanage of the French crown a fresh source of

PONTIFF: *pope*
APPANAGE: *extension*

wealth would be added to his revenue; and for these material gifts he was quite willing to let Pope Innocent appoint what bishops he pleased to rule in the Church of France, or change the ritual, and add a few more doctrines for his subjects to believe in.

So the news was soon wafted across the sea that King Philip was collecting a formidable army to invade England, and that, strengthened by the pope's command and blessing, he expected to gain an easy victory.

This thoroughly aroused John's fears. He at once dispatched an envoy to propitiate Pope Innocent and promise his submission, and then set about his preparations to resist his old enemy. It was easier to collect an army to resist Philip than that monarch supposed, knowing, as he doubtless did, that John was cordially hated by his subjects, and they would gladly have seen him destroyed.

But the dethronement of John meant England's subjugation to France, and the English knew that their land would then be drained of its resources, taxes imposed, and commerce checked, merely that France might be enriched. The loss of Normandy, Anjou, and the other continental provinces which had been the hereditary right of each sovereign since the conquering William had won the English crown, had been a severe blow to the national pride; but men were beginning to learn that it was not an unmitigated misfortune, for the money lavished in Normandy was now circulating

WAFTED: *floated*
PROPITIATE: *gain the favor of*

in England, and she was beginning to have an independent life, instead of being a mere appanage of these larger territorial possessions. All these considerations helped John very materially, and he had soon collected an army of sixty thousand men, and sent forth the Cinque Ports' fleet, which destroyed several French vessels.

The English army was encamped near Dover, to be in readiness for the landing of Philip, when John's messenger to Rome returned, and with him the papal legate, Pandulph, to receive his promised submission.

The legate was most successful in arousing the cowardly monarch's fears concerning the resources of Philip and the certainty of his success, and that the only way to secure himself from the impending danger was to place himself under the protection of the pontiff.

John's submission was as abject as his obstinacy had been determined. In the Temple Church of Dover he kneeled down in the sight of his assembled barons and soldiers, and, with his hands between the legate's, solemnly repeated this oath:

"I, John, by the grace of God king of England and lord of Ireland, in order to expiate my sins, from my own free will and the advice of my barons give to the Church of Rome, to Pope Innocent and his successors, the kingdom of England and all other prerogatives of my crown. I will hereafter hold them as the pope's vassal. I will be faithful to God, to the Church of Rome, and to the pope, my

SUBJUGATION: *becoming subject*
PREROGATIVES: *rights and privileges*

master, and his successors. I promise to pay him a tribute of a thousand marks yearly, to wit: seven hundred for the kingdom of England, and three hundred for the kingdom of Ireland."

Langton, the Archbishop of Canterbury, was also to be received, as well as all the bishops who had been banished by John, and the Church property was all to be restored. Thus in the selfsame day was England sold, and the champion of her liberty ignominiously thrust upon her. Had Pope Innocent only known Stephen Langton as the stern, indomitable Englishman he proved to be, he would rather have made the stipulation that he should never be allowed to enter his native land again. But the craftiest politicians overreach themselves sometimes, as the pope did in this appointment.

After receiving John's submission, and keeping his resigned crown three days, the papal legate restored it in the name of his master, and withdrew the excommunication and interdict, promising also that Philip of France should not be allowed to disturb the peace of England. The barons returned home rather sulky, as well as more disgusted with John, for they each felt that they were but pawns on the chessboard of Europe, and could be moved by the master-hand of the pope at his will, and there was a deeper determination than ever to assert their claim to liberty now that England was reduced to vassalage by her king.

The feeling that had been slowly growing, however, smoldered on for two years longer, and might

INDOMITABLE: *unconquerable*

not have burst forth into action when it did had not the king tried to force his barons to engage in a war he chose to declare against France. This they refused to do, and met in a council at St. Alban's, and resolved that the laws of Henry I should be observed.

Guy was still living at Northampton, and the young archdeacon, Grosseteste, was busy reforming various abuses that came under his care, preaching from the Gospel itself instead of teaching the legends of the saints, so that Guy began to indulge the hope that his beloved land might yet be rescued from the tyrannical power of Rome, more especially as Langton had promised to help the barons in their struggle for liberty.

Never until now had Guy regretted the loss of his inheritance; but it was a sore trial when a second meeting was called in the Church of St. Paul's, London, where the archbishop boldly came forward and read the great charter of Henry, and administered to those present an oath, binding them to conquer or die in the defense of their liberties.

There was a humble cheapman among the crowd of citizens who thronged the back of the church, who as devoutly took that vow in his heart as any baron, and was at his brother's side in every emergency and moment of vacillation, for it was a perilous adventure in which they were now engaged; and at a third meeting held at Bury St. Edmunds, each baron took an oath upon the altar to withdraw his allegiance from King John should

VACILLATION: *indecision*

he reject their claims. Their demands were presented to the king early in January, 1215, and they were promised an answer at Easter.

But the barons had little doubt as to what this was likely to be by the measures the king at once began to set on foot. To gain the goodwill of the clergy—many of whom were foreigners—he granted them at once the charter of free election. He then ordered the sheriffs to take the oath of allegiance to his person from every free man; enrolled himself as a crusader; and hired mercenaries from Flanders to subdue his refractory subjects should they side with the barons.

Both parties sent off their envoys to Rome. Pope Innocent preferred to side with the king, and sent a letter to Archbishop Langton, blaming him as the mover of this sedition, and commanding him to make peace between the contending parties. This, however, he could not do as required. He therefore determined to adhere to the oath he had administered to the barons, though it cost him the friendship of the pontiff and the loss of his see.

As had been expected, John sought by evasion to get rid of the troublesome claims brought before him; but the measures of the barons, though of slow growth, were of giant strength. So, conscious of their power, the barons at once threatened, and even commenced, hostilities by taking London. This brought the king to terms, and the two parties agreed to meet at a little islet called

SET ON FOOT: *set into place*

Runnymede, between Staines and Windsor.

John was accompanied by eight bishops and a few gentlemen, who had a small camp on one side, while on the other were pitched the pavilions of nearly all England's noblemen, with the Archbishop of Canterbury at their head. Brave, true-hearted Stephen Langton, he had all to lose and nothing to gain by thus stepping forward as the champion of English liberty, and well might the barons be proud and confident with such a man to lead them.

Again the humble cheapman was near, hovering about the pavilions; and if he had been closely watched, he might have been seen to retire more than once to a little shady dell—not to look over his pack and count his gains, but to pour out his heart in prayer to God that this first effort to gain something like liberty for his country might be successful. Not that men so humble as Guy Ericson would gain much by it just yet. It was for the de Valerys and other proud nobles to profit by this, but it was a beginning, Guy thought, and by and by the blessing would come down on all classes of the community, until at length the lowest and poorest might claim as his right what the proudest baron had been made to feel lately he only held at the king's pleasure—the liberty to hold or sell property at their own will, and that they should not be cast into prison or outlawed except by judgment of their peers, according to the law of the land. In

SHADY DELL: *small, wooded valley*

many a castle home, too, there were prayers being
offered by wives and mothers and sisters, who had
buckled on the armor, and sent forth their dearest to win or die for this liberty; but none were
more true or earnest than rose from a little retired
home near Northampton Abbey.

There were only two women here; but two more
earnest souls lived not in England: for one had witnessed scenes that struck a chill of horror to her
even now, and the other was fast tasting of that liberty wherewith Christ makes His people free, and
looking back upon that bitter bondage in which
she had lived for years. She too, therefore, longed
that others might know and be free to proclaim
the blessed Gospel message of salvation without
fear.

To the intense joy of Elfreda and Lady de Valery,
Guy returned almost sooner than he was expected, bringing with him the good news that the king
had signed the Great Charter,[1] which must prove
the foundation of English liberty; and the next day,
closely wrapped in mufflers, they went with Guy to
hear it read to the vast crowd who had assembled
in the marketplace to hear it. But neither of the
women heard more than the first clause: "That the
Church of England shall be free, and enjoy her
whole rights and privileges inviolable." There were
seventy-two clauses, each necessary, Guy said, to
protect those to whom they referred from extor-
tion and oppression. The Church, the barons, the

---

[1] *Magna Charta*

INVIOLABLE: *without them being violated*

merchants, and freemen generally, would be protected by this charter, but for the rest of the people they were little better than slaves at present. The Great Charter was a beginning; the days of free and equal rights for all were yet to come.

And here we must leave our humble Saxon family. In the quiet years that followed no one of the three seemed for a moment to regret the rank and greatness which might have been their lot. Lady de Valery before she ended her days found the blessedness of a simple trust in Christ. Priest and confessor gradually discontinued their visits to that quiet abode; and though Sir Guy eventually became rich and powerful, through circumstances that we have no space to narrate, his happiest rememberances were of the days spent in that lowly home, when his tenderly beloved wife, now known as the Good Lady Elfreda, had been as an angel of mercy by his mother's side. The seed sown long, long before by Leofwine in that monastery among the fens had yielded a hundred-fold in the lives of these unconscious REFORMERS BEFORE THE REFORMATION.

The End

ABOUT THE AUTHOR

Emma Leslie (1837-1909), whose actual name was Emma Dixon, lived in Lewisham, Kent, in the south of England. She was a prolific Victorian children's author who wrote over 100 books. Emma Leslie's first book, *The Two Orphans*, was published in 1863 and her books remained in print for years after her death. She is buried at the St. Mary's Parish Church, in Pwllcrochan, Pembroke, South Wales.

Emma Leslie brought a strong Christian emphasis into her writing and many of her books were published by the Religious Tract Society. Her extensive historical fiction works covered many important periods in church history. Her writing also included a short booklet on the life of Queen Victoria published in the 50th year of the Queen's reign.

EMMA LESLIE CHURCH HISTORY SERIES

GLAUCIA THE GREEK SLAVE
A Tale of Athens in the First Century

After the death of her father, Glaucia is sold to a wealthy Roman family to pay his debts. She tries hard to adjust to her new life but longs to find a God who can love even a slave. Meanwhile, her brother, Laon, struggles to find her and to earn enough money to buy her freedom. But what is the mystery that surrounds their mother's disappearance years earlier and will they ever be able to read the message in the parchments she left for them?

THE CAPTIVES
Or, Escape from the Druid Council

The Druid priests are as cold and cruel as the forest spirits they claim to represent, and Guntra, the chief of her tribe of Britons, must make a desperate deal with them to protect those she loves. Unaware of Guntra's struggles, Jugurtha, her son, longs to drive the hated Roman conquerors from the land. When he encounters the Christian centurion, Marcinius, Jugurtha mocks the idea of a God of love and kindness, but there comes a day when he is in need of love and kindness for himself and his beloved little sister. Will he allow Marcinius to help him? And will the gospel of Jesus Christ ever penetrate the brutal religion of the proud Britons?

www.SalemRidgePress.com

EMMA LESLIE CHURCH HISTORY SERIES

OUT OF THE MOUTH OF THE LION
Or, The Church in the Catacombs

When Flaminius, a high Roman official, takes his wife, Flavia, to the Colosseum to see Christians thrown to the lions, he has no idea the effect it will have. Flavia cannot forget the faith of the martyrs, and finally, to protect her from complete disgrace or even danger, Flaminius requests a transfer to a more remote government post. As he and his family travel to the seven cities of Asia Minor mentioned in Revelation, he sees the various responses of the churches to persecution. His attitude toward the despised Christians begins to change, but does he dare forsake the gods of Rome and embrace the Lord Jesus Christ?

SOWING BESIDE ALL WATERS
A Tale of the World in the Church

There is newfound freedom from persecution for Christians under the emperor, Constantine, but newfound troubles as well. Errors and pagan ways are creeping into the Church, while many of the most devoted Christians are withdrawing from the world into the desert as hermits and nuns. Quadratus, one of the emperor's special guards, is concerned over these developments, even in his own family. Then a riot sweeps through the city and Quadratus' home is ransacked. When he regains consciousness, he finds that his sister, Placidia, is gone. Where is she? And can the Church handle the new freedom, and remain faithful?

www.SalemRidgePress.com

Emma Leslie Church History Series

FROM BONDAGE TO FREEDOM
A Tale of the Times of Mohammed

At a Syrian market two Christian women are sold as slaves. One of the slaves ends up in Rome where Bishop Gregory is teaching his new doctrine of "purgatory" and the need for Christians to finish paying for their own sins. The other slave travels with her new master, Mohammed, back to Arabia, where Mohammed eventually declares himself to be the prophet of God. In Rome and Arabia, the two women and countless others fall into the bondage of man-made religions—will they learn at last to find true freedom in the Lord Jesus Christ alone?

THE MARTYR'S VICTORY
A Story of Danish England

Knowing full well they may die in the attempt, a small band of monks sets out to convert the savage Danes who have laid waste to the surrounding countryside year after year. The monks' faith is sorely tested as they face opposition from the angry Priest of Odin as well as doubts, sickness and starvation, but their leader, Osric, is unwavering in his attempts to share the "White Christ" with those who reject Him. Then the monks discover a young Christian woman who has escaped being sacrificed to the Danish gods—can she help reach those who had enslaved her and tried to kill her?

GYTHA'S MESSAGE
A Tale of Saxon England

Having discovered God's love for her, Gytha, a young slave, longs to escape the violence and cruelty of the world and devote herself to learning more about this God of love. Instead she lives in a Saxon household that despises the name of Christ. Her simple faith and devoted service bring hope and purpose to those around her, especially during the dark days when England is defeated by William the Conqueror. Through all of her trials, can Gytha learn to trust that God often has greater work for us to do *in* the world than *out* of it?

www.SalemRidgePress.com

Emma Leslie Church History Series

LEOFWINE THE MONK
Or, The Curse of the Ericsons
A Story of a Saxon Family

Leofwine, unlike his wild, younger brother, finds no pleasure in terrorizing the countrside, and longs to enter a monastery. Shortly after he does, however, he hears strange rumors of a monk who preaches "heresy". Unable to stop thinking about these new ideas, Leofwine at last determines to leave the monastery and England. Leofwine's search for inner peace takes him to France and Rome and finally to Jerusalem, but in his travels, he uncovers a plot against his beloved country. Will he be able to help save England? And will he ever find true rest for his troubled soul?

ELFREDA THE SAXON
Or, The Orphan of Jerusalem
A Sequel to Leofwine

When Jerusalem is captured by the Muslims, Elfreda, a young orphan, is sent back to England to her mother's sister. Her aunt is not at all pleased to see her, and her uncle fears she may have brought the family curse back to England. Elfreda's cousin, Guy, who is joining King Richard's Crusade, promises Elfreda that he will win such honor as a crusader that the curse will be removed. Over the years that follow, however, severe trials befall the family and Guy and Elfreda despair of the curse ever being lifted. Is it possible that there is One with power stronger than any curse?

DEARER THAN LIFE
A Story of the Times of Wycliffe

When a neighboring monastery lays claim to one of his fields, Sir Hugh Middleton refuses to yield his property, and further offends the monastery by sending his younger son, Stephen, to study under Dr. John Wycliffe. At the same time, Sir Hugh sends his elder son, Harry, to serve as an attendant to the powerful Duke of Lancaster. As Wycliffe seeks to share the Word of God with the common people, Stephen and Harry and their sisters help spread the truth, but what will it cost them in the dangerous day in which they live?

www.SalemRidgePress.com

Emma Leslie Church History Series

BEFORE THE DAWN
A Tale of Wycliffe and Huss

To please her crippled grandson, Conrad, Dame Ursula allows a kindly blacksmith and his friend, Ned Trueman, to visit the boy. Soon, however, she becomes suspicious that the men belong to the despised group who are followers of Dr. John Wycliffe, and she passionately warns Conrad of the dangers of evil "heresy". He decides to become a famous teacher in the Church so he can combat heresy, but he wonders why all the remedies of the Church fail to cure him. And why do his mother and grandmother refuse to speak of the father he has never known?

FAITHFUL, BUT NOT FAMOUS
A Tale of the French Reformation

Young Claude Leclerc travels to Paris to begin his training for the priesthood, but he is not sure *what* he believes about God. One day he learns the words to an old hymn and is drawn to the lines about "David's Royal Fountain" that will "purge every sin away." Claude yearns to find this fountain, and at last dares to ask the famous Dr. Lefèvre where he can find it. His question leads Dr. Lefèvre to set aside his study of the saints and study the Scriptures in earnest. As Dr. Lefèvre grasps the wonderful truth of salvation by grace, he wants to share it with Claude, but Claude has mysteriously disappeared. Where is he? And is France truly ready to receive the good news of the gospel of Jesus Christ?

www.SalemRidgePress.com

Church History for Younger Readers

SOLDIER FRITZ
A Story of the Reformation
by Emma Leslie
Illustrated by C. A. Ferrier

Young Fritz wants to follow in the footsteps of Martin Luther and be a soldier for the Lord, so he chooses a Bible from the peddler's pack as his birthday gift. When his father, the Count, goes off to war, however, Fritz and his mother and little sister are forced to flee into the forest to escape being thrown in prison for their new faith. Disguising themselves as commoners, they must trust the Lord as they wait and hope for the Count to rescue them. But how will he ever be able to find them?

www.SalemRidgePress.com

Additional Titles Available From

Salem Ridge Press

DOWN THE SNOW STAIRS
Or, From Goodnight to Goodmorning
by Alice Corkran
Illustrated by Gordon Browne R. I.

On Christmas Eve, eight-year-old Kitty cannot sleep, know-ing that her beloved little brother is critically ill due to her own disobedience. Traveling in a dream to Naughty Children Land, she meets many strange people, including Daddy Coax and Lady Love. Kitty longs to return to the Path of Obedience but can she resist the many temptations she faces? Will she find her way home in time for Christmas? An imaginative and delightful read-aloud for the whole family!

YOUNG ROBIN HOOD
by George Manville Fenn
Illustrated by Victor Venner

In the days of Robin Hood, a young boy named Robin is journey-ing through Sherwood Forest when suddenly the company is surrounded by men in green. Deserted in the commotion by an unfaithful servant, Robin finds himself alone in the for-est. After a miserable night, Robin is found by Little John. Robin is treated kindly by Robin Hood, Maid Marian and the Merry Men, but how long must he wait for his father, the Sheriff of Nottingham, to come to take him home?

www.SalemRidgePress.com

Fiction for Younger Readers

MARY JANE – HER BOOK
by Clara Ingram Judson
Illustrated by Francis White

This story, the first book in the Mary Jane series, recounts the happy, wholesome adventures of five-year-old Mary Jane and her family as she helps her mother around the house, goes on a picnic with the big girls, plants a garden with her father, learns to sew and more!

MARY JANE – HER VISIT
by Clara Ingram Judson
Illustrated by Francis White

In this story, the second book in the Mary Jane series, five-year-old Mary Jane has more happy, wholesome adventures, this time at her great-grandparents' farm in the country where she hunts for eggs, picks berries, finds baby rabbits, goes to the circus and more!

www.SalemRidgePress.com

Historical Fiction for Younger Readers

AMERICAN TWINS OF THE REVOLUTION
by Lucy Fitch Perkins

General Washington has no money to pay his discouraged troops and twins Sally and Roger are asked by their father, General Priestly, to help hide a shipment of gold which will be used to pay the American soldiers. Unfortunately, British spies have also learned about the gold and will stop at nothing to prevent it from reaching General Washington. Based on a true story, this is a thrilling episode from our nation's history!

MARIE'S HOME
Or, A Glimpse of the Past
by Caroline Austin
Illustrated by Gordon Browne R. I.

Eleven-year-old Marie Hamilton and her family travel to France at the invitation of Louis XVI, just before the start of the French Revolution. There they encounter the tremendous disparity between the proud French Nobility and the oppressed and starving French people. When an enraged mob storms the palace of Versailles, Marie and her family are rescued from grave danger by a strange twist of events, but Marie's story of courage, self-sacrifice and true nobility is not yet over! Honor, duty, compassion and forgiveness are all portrayed in this uplifting story.

www.SalemRidgePress.com

Historical Fiction by William W. Canfield

THE WHITE SENECA
Illustrated by G. A. Harker

Captured by the Senecas, fifteen-year-old Henry Cochrane grows to love the Indian ways and becomes Dundiswa—the White Seneca. When Henry is captured by an enemy tribe, however, he must make a desperate attempt to escape from them and rescue fellow captive, Constance Leonard. He will need all the skills he has learned from the Indians, as well as great courage and determination, if he is to succeed. But what will happen to the young woman if they do reach safety? And will he ever be able to return to his own people?

AT SENECA CASTLE
Illustrated by G. A. Harker

In this sequel to *The White Seneca*, Henry Cochrane, now eighteen, faces many perils as he serves as a scout for the Continental Army. General Washington is determined to do whatever it takes to stop the constant Indian attacks on the settlers and yet Henry is torn between his love for the Senecas and his loyalty to his own people. As the Army advances across New York State, Henry receives permission to travel ahead and warn his Indian friends of the coming destruction. But will he reach them in time? And what has happened to the beautiful Constance Leonard whom he had been forced to leave in captivity a year earlier?

THE SIGN ABOVE THE DOOR

Young Prince Martiesen is ruler of the land of Goshen in Egypt, where the Hebrews live. Eight plagues have already come upon Egypt and now Martiesen has been forced by Pharaoh to further increase the burden of the Hebrews. Martiesen, however, is in love with the beautiful Hebrew maiden, Elisheba, whom he is forbidden by Egyptian law to marry. As the nation despairs, the other nobles turn to Martiesen for leadership, but before he can decide what to do, Elisheba is kidnapped by the evil Peshala and terrifying darkness falls over the land. An exciting tale woven around the events of the Exodus from the Egyptian perspective!

www.SalemRidgePress.com

Adventure by George Manville Fenn

YUSSUF THE GUIDE
*Being the Strange Story of the Travels in Asia Minor of
Burne the Lawyer, Preston the Professor, and
Lawrence the Sick*
Illustrated by John Schönberg

Young Lawrence, an invalid, convinces his guardians, Preston the Professor and Burne the Lawyer, to take him along on an archaeological expedition to Turkey. Before they set out, they engage Yussuf as their guide. Through the months that follow, the friends travel deeper and deeper into the remote regions of central Turkey on their trusty horses in search of ancient ruins. Yussuf proves his worth time and time again as they face dangers from a murderous ship captain, poisonous snakes, sheer precipices, bands of robbers and more. Memorable characters, humor and adventure abound in this exciting story!

www.SalemRidgePress.com

CPSIA information can be obtained at www.ICGtesting.com
Printed in the USA
LVOW051256181212

312177LV00001B/10/P